SAGE

GUARDIAN DEFENDERS

KRIS MICHAELS

WWW.KRISMICHAELSAUTHOR.COM

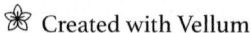

1

Sage Browning knew the winding roads of Plaquemines Parish like the back of his hand. He'd grown up there, and because he knew all the hiding places and speed traps of the local cops, he sure as hell hadn't been speeding. Yet, the flashing blue lights in his rearview mirror and the lack of other traffic on the pothole-strewn road leading into Bienvenu told him nothing had changed. Out-of-state plates were always targeted. Easy money because no one wanted to come back to fight the tickets.

Sage signaled his intent to pull over, slowed, guided his truck to the side of the road, and pulled out his driver's license, concealed carry permit, and Guardian shield. Even though he was on word responses and vowels were better than consonants for him.

"Man, sorry to hear that. Yeah, I heard from my pop that Gus was found wandering one night. Your mom went out, sick like she is, and took him home. He won't be happy you're back. Not like that old bastard is happy about anything, ever. Your brothers coming to help?"

Sage shook his head. "N-no." His half-brothers were scattered to the far corners of the earth. They offered to send Sage money for their mom's medical expenses, and they called her religiously, but Sage told them not to come. He'd always protected his younger brothers. Seth, Kevin, and Carter all loved their momma, but coming back meant being around Gus and the rest of the people in Bienvenu. The people who looked down on the "bastard brothers," as they were called growing up.

Sage was probably the only one of the four who wouldn't kill Gus. Words were Gus' weapon of choice for him. Gus had ignored and humiliated him, but he'd beaten the younger kids. Somehow Gus had it in his head that it was legal to "discipline" *his* kids. Sage wasn't his. He was only two years old when the mean bastard appeared in his

"The Chevy." Sage laughed. Damn, that old piece of rust was held together with fishing line and a prayer.

"We got it running." Beau laughed. They'd spent all summer of their sophomore year working on the hunk of junk. Beau's dad had been a saint and ridiculously patient as he taught both boys how to troubleshoot mechanical issues. Sage and his brothers had spent most of their free time at the Theriot's. Beau's parents would feed them, not that they had much, but Mrs. T. could stretch whatever she had so they had enough. Beau's dad had a shrimp boat, and as the boys aged, they worked on the shrimper. It was almost a right of passage.

"A sh-sheriff?" Sage asked when they stopped laughing.

Beau sighed. "Yeah. I went to LSU on that football scholarship. Blew out my knee my senior year. I was a mess. I'd be a drunk living on Canal Street if it wasn't for Evangeline." Beau held up his hand, showing off the glowing gold band on his ring finger.

"No." Sage smiled at his friend. Evangeline Thibodeaux was a firecracker as a young girl and the most beautiful girl in the parish. "You?"

"Yeah, me. What? You don't think I could land that woman?"

"Why would sh-she want you?" Sage ducked a swipe his friend sent his way.

"Shut up, man, or I'm not inviting you for Sunday dinner. You need to meet the kids, and my mom and dad would kick my backside if I didn't bring you by."

Sage's mouth dropped open. "K-kids?"

"Yep. A boy and a girl. Sage and Selene."

Sage blinked at his friend. "Wow."

"Don't let it go to your head." Beau rolled his eyes and quickly tipped his head toward his radio as it squawked something unintelligible. "Listen, I got to go check in, but I'll swing by the Bait Shop. I know those two assholes will start something.

"They can s-start it." He'd finish it.

"I know you can handle yourself, but remember where you are, my friend. Don't throw the first punch."

"Never." Sage extended his hand, clasping Beau's.

"That means don't kill no one either. I'd hate to arrest you on your first night home. My pappy would tan my ass." Beau spoke with humor, but Sage knew the man would do his job, even if it meant arresting Sage. "I'll swing by the house tomorrow before my shift." Beau held up his free hand. "Don't tell me not to do it. I like your momma. Gus can take a flying leap if he doesn't like me being on his property."

Sage nodded and got back into his truck. He glanced at the clock and smiled. He wanted a drink before he faced the mess his life had put in front of him. Not that he needed the liquid courage. He didn't drink much at all. What he wanted was to put the town on notice. He was back, and he wasn't the kid who had run from Bienvenu at the first opportunity.

The drive to the Bait Shop was a short one. Sage parked his truck and locked it, dropping the key fob into his jacket. As he stepped out and walked to the entrance, his black combat boots crunched through the gravel. The Bait Shop hadn't changed, he noted once he'd gone inside. Hell, it hadn't changed in all the time he'd lived there. The block building's three windows were boarded up, always prepared for the hurricanes threatening the area. The inside was bare-bones basics only. A cooler, a tap with three beer kegs kept cold in a unit under the bar, and two long shelves with whiskey, vodka, and not much more. There were bagged chips and peanuts for those who wanted to pay. One television sat on the opposite wall from a dartboard. The jukebox that had been there when he grew up had been a casualty of one of the hurricanes that blew through. Sage didn't remember which hurricane.

Now, however, there were wireless speakers up in the corners of the room and country music pouring out of them. Three tables had people sitting at them. He knew where Bergeron and Broussard were sitting by the obnoxious language coming from the farthest table. He paid them no attention and headed for the bar. Old Man Ladner made his way to the end of the bar and stared at him. "Been a long time."

Sage nodded. "B-Bourbon."

Ladner glanced over at the far table. "You looking for a fight?"

Sage shook his head. He wasn't looking for one, but he wouldn't run from one either. Ladner's bushy eyebrows lifted toward the ceiling, but he didn't say anything else. Grabbing a glass, he poured Sage a drink. Sage pulled out his wallet and dropped a twenty on the bar.

"Well, well, well, if it isn't one of the Bienvenu Bastard Brothers. What the hell are you doing back here?" Gary Bergeron's voice was loud and obnoxious.

Sage put his wallet in his pocket, lifted his middle finger without turning around, and flew the bird at his childhood bully.

The sound of chairs scraping on the cement floor wasn't unexpected. "Care to repeat that?"

Sage glanced at Old Man Ladner and smiled, lifting his finger again. Ladner rolled his eyes and backed away from where Sage was leaning against the bar.

He felt the hand land on his shoulder and pivoted on his heel, spinning faster than Bergeron expected. The man's eyes widened. "Look at you. Lots of jewelry, faggot."

Sage lifted his hand. Three heavy silver rings delivered one hell of a punch when he formed a fist. He also wore a silver chain and cross around his neck. "S-so"

"What? Is the sissy scared? He's stuttering." Bergeron pointed at him and hooted.

Broussard laughed and took a step forward. "Maybe we should remind him that his type isn't wanted around here."

"M-my type?" He knew what the man meant. Those guys had terrorized him for as long as he could remember. Gus had called him a sissy-boy in front of them once, and they'd taken it to extremes. Thank God he'd left that backwater hole. He wasn't bisexual or gay, but he didn't give two thoughts about whom a person slept with or loved. It shouldn't matter to anyone. Except people like those two narrow-minded bigots always cared.

"Yeah, a queer," Bergeron added as if Sage needed the explanation.

Sage smiled and then winked at Broussard before he pursed his lips in a kiss. That was the ignition point. Broussard had always been the hot head. The man lunged at Sage, who sidestepped to his right and ducked the bull rush. Bergeron moved quickly, ramming a poorly aimed fist at Sage.

Sage caught the bastard's fist in his hand and pulled it past him, coming up behind Bergeron and locking the man's arm behind his back. Sage jacked the fist up almost far enough to pop the man's shoulder out of the socket. Damn, to think he used to kowtow to these fucktards. A howl of frustration from Bergeron, who had lifted onto his toes to lessen the pressure, brought Broussard to his feet. Sage saw the confusion on Broussard's face. He lifted his arm a bit farther, heightening the tension, and Bergeron howled again. Broussard grabbed a chair and hefted it skyward. Sage ducked behind Bergeron, who took the brunt of the blow. He let go of the man's fist when he felt the shoulder go with a sickening pop.

Broussard grabbed Sage's jacket. Sage slipped out of it and held the sleeves like he'd been taught. He wrapped the material around Brossard's arm and spun, twisting the man like a pretzel. Then Sage pulled the jacket up, locking Broussard's arm behind him, just as he had Bergeron's. "Not your p-punching bag, n-not your b-bitch." Sage lifted the sleeves of his jacket, and Broussard screamed when his shoulder dislocated. Sage unwrapped his leather jacket as quickly and efficiently as he'd coiled it around the man's arm. He draped the leather over the barstool next to him and reached for his bourbon.

"I'm pressing charges," Bergeron groaned from the floor. Good to know the chair hadn't knocked him out.

"For what?" Old Man Ladner chuckled. "You started it, and your friend slammed you with a chair."

"I got witnesses." Bergeron held his arm as he tried to stand.

"So does Sage. You're damn lucky I don't want to do paperwork tonight, or I'd be taking you in for disorderly conduct. It's beyond stupid to take on a federal officer. Don't you know Sage is a Fed now?" Beau spoke from where he stood in the doorway. Sage glanced at him and lifted his bourbon to his lips as Old Man Ladner's head snapped in Beau's direction. His friend had given him credibility. He didn't need it or want it from that town, but still, the taste of the rotgut whiskey he'd been served was the sweetest thing he'd had in years. Sage had served himself a big ole helping of ice-cold revenge. It tasted damn good.

Ladner poured him a second drink as Beau sorted out the trash on the floor. "They've been running roughshod over people around here forever. Glad to see someone take them down a peg without even throwing a punch." The old man cackled. "This time tomorrow, they won't be able to show their faces without people knowing you'd had enough of their shit. You're welcome here anytime, officer."

Sage downed the second drink and grabbed his jacket. He sent a two-finger salute to the bartender and walked out the door—time to go home.

2

P*resent day, almost a year after the Siege:*

HONOR BUCHANAN POURED vodka into her tumbler. The orange juice had run out sometime yesterday. She didn't care. Since the day she'd landed in Dallas a year ago, she'd been drinking. At first, it was to calm her nerves. She'd left DC after emptying her savings account and had covered her tracks while leaving. She'd used cash for everything, leaving no digital footprint. To ensure she was safe, she'd hacked into every truck stop she'd stopped at, wiping out any video imagery of her face. Losing herself in Dallas, she'd found an apartment near a liquor store and deleted her many trips from the store's camera ... when she was sober enough to remember to do it.

Jewell had found her three days ago when she'd accessed her bank account to liquidate investments after running out of money. Or was it four days? Maybe five. She didn't fucking care. But Jewell had been persistent. Honor hadn't answered any of the attempts at communication. She'd been using a burner phone, but she had her Guardian cell powered up now. She wouldn't put it past Jewell to send a team to find her if she didn't.

Her phone rang beside her computer. Honor leaned over and looked at the face of the phone. She huffed and swiped to connect the call. Before she could say a word, Jewell, her boss, spoke, "Why are you hiding? Why haven't you answered before this?"

Honor snorted and took a hit of the vodka. "Why do you care?"

"What?" Jewell's voice held a bit of hurt in the tone.

Damn it. Honor dropped her head back on the couch. "I'm not hiding from *you*." Much. There were others she prayed wouldn't find her. But if

Jewell had tracked her down, it would only be time before a lesser skilled person could find her, too. She didn't have it in her to run farther. She was done. Done running. Done hiding. She took another sip of the vodka.

"Why are you acting this way, Honor? Is it because of what happened?"

Honor froze with the glass halfway to her lips. "What?"

"The attack. It messed with all of us. You know we can get you some help."

Honor blinked at the phone. God, if the explosion was her only problem. "I can't sleep." She blurted the words out, and it was true. Unless she was totally blotto—then she could fall asleep. Staying asleep or not having nightmares wasn't guaranteed, even if she was three sheets to the wind.

"We can help you with that. I can send someone to bring you home," Jewell offered her help again.

Honor huffed and reached for the vodka bottle, stopping with it halfway to her glass. She admitted, almost to herself, "The explosion isn't the only thing, Jewell. I'm so fucked." She poured another inch of vodka into her glass. "So fuckedy-fucked."

It wasn't funny, but she laughed anyway. "I should have died in that explosion. I should've been killed. I should be in one of those graves." It would have been poetic justice, wouldn't it?

"Why would you say something like that? Honor, coming back to Guardian will help no matter how bad things seem. We have counselors, people who can help."

"Help?" Honor shook her head. "You have no idea what I'm talking about. How can you help?"

"I would know if you opened up to me. Come back. No matter what thoughts are running around inside, Guardian will help you bring everything into the light where you can look at it. I've had help. I've been where you are, Honor."

"No, you've never been where I am." She looked at her main computer. Such a stupid mistake from an impressionable young girl. God, she'd aged a lifetime in the years since that incident. But her past had found her, hadn't it? She shook her head. Jewell wasn't like her. Jewell was confident and beautiful and had a husband who adored her. Honor had nothing. Less than nothing. God, she'd tried so damn hard to make up for the mistake she'd made all those years ago, but just as she knew it would, her past had circled around to snap her in the ass. If she went back to Guardian ... Wait ... Honor blinked and grabbed for the phone that was more than a little fuzzy. Suppose she told them who and when, well, no ... who and why, not when ... but if they knew, she'd be in jail. A person could go to jail for what she did ...

Maybe she could sleep in a cell. A cell sounded good right then. Iron bars kept people out. No computers, no problems. Damn. No alcohol. *That* could be a problem. She took another drink and rolled her head toward the phone. "Can I tell you something, Jewell, something you might not know about me?"

"Is it that you're drinking vodka?"

Honor blinked at the phone and then looked up at her secondary computer. The green light on the camera was illuminated. She leaned back and stared at the blank screen. "Didn't take you long."

"Once I had a fix on your cell, it was child's play." Jewell chuckled. "You know that."

"Hmmm ..." She did know that. She lifted the vodka bottle straight to her lips and took a long swig. "That's not what I wanted to tell you." Her face was feeling numb. Oh, that was good. Numb came before sleep. Sleep, she so wanted to sleep.

"Honor?"

She blinked up and looked at the computer. It was wavering back and forth a bit. "Huh?"

"What did you want to tell me?" Jewell asked.

Honor frowned. "What?" She looked at her phone again. What had she wanted to tell Jewell? She couldn't remember. "You sound close."

"Nope, far away. My new office is the best."

"Not ever going back to an office building." Honor hugged the bottle of vodka and lay down, talking into the couch's cushion. Maybe she could sleep for a little bit.

"I didn't understand that." Jewell's voice was getting farther away. "Can I send someone to get you?"

Honor lifted her head a bit to talk. "Said, never going back to a building. Office. Why do you care?" Even to her ears, her words were slurred. So damn tired. She reached over and closed the laptop, stopping the video feed to Jewell.

"Because you're my friend," Jewell replied. "I don't have many left. I know you're hurting. Let me help you."

Honor closed her eyes and turned her head, so she wasn't talking into the sofa any longer. "You won't like me when you know." Honor shook her head, but it made her dizzy, so she stopped. She was responsible for all of it. How could she go back?

"I'll always like you, Honor. I'm sending someone to pick you up and take you somewhere you can get help. Okay?"

Honor sighed. What had Jewell said? Something about help. She could help Jewell in the morning.

"Okay."

"You said okay?"

Did she? She didn't know. But she nodded and agreed again because she'd always liked Jewell. "Yeah, okay. Night." Honor closed her eyes and let the darkness take over.

JEWELL LEANED back in her chair. The office inside her mountain was warm and built to her exact specifications. She pushed the floor with her toe and spun around to her husband, who was watching her. "She's going to kill herself drinking like that."

"You can't save those who don't want to be saved, Jewell."

"She said yes."

"She was almost passed out," Zane reminded her.

"Well, true, but I have consent, and I recorded it." Jewell slid out of her chair and went over to sit on her husband's lap. He wrapped his big arms around her, and she leaned into him. "Whatever happened to her is a result of that damn explosion. She was one of the few who got out of the auditorium."

"She has a problem. It could be a long time before she can work again."

"I don't care. She deserves a chance and some help." Jewell sighed. "She's like me, you know. Awkward."

"You aren't awkward. You process things differently, that's all." Zane kissed her on the temple.

"You see that and explain the world to me. Who does it for Honor?" Jewell looked up at him. "We need to send someone to take her to get help."

Zane nodded. "We have our Thursday staff meeting in three minutes. We'll bring it up then, but you were going to do that anyway."

Nobody wanted Friday staff meetings anymore, so Jason moved the weekly meeting to Thursday. Jewell smiled at her husband. "Yeah. I was."

"I figured. You need to get the call started." He

kissed her and sighed when she slipped off his lap to start the secure conference. "Have you found any changes you want to make to the office setup? I'm running into town on Saturday."

Jewell pulled a pencil from her messy bun and shook her head as she gazed around at the state-of-the-art system installed in their new home. "No. Everything I need is right here in front of me."

"Everything?" Zane asked from behind her.

Jewell stopped and looked at the equipment that surrounded her. "Ah ..."

Zane dropped a kiss on top of her head. She looked up at him, and realization dawned on her. "Everything except you."

"Right answer." Zane winked at her and entered the room Lycos had used as a vault. She and Zane had removed the massive door and renovated the space for video conferences.

Once Jewell had made the conference call to the department heads and the CEO of Guardian Security and ensured the links were secure, she moved into the room with Zane and sat beside him.

Her brothers Jacob and Joseph signed on first. "Hey, Button," Joseph greeted, smiling at her. "How's life in the wild?"

"Wonderful." She beamed. "We're getting a puppy."

"What kind?" Jacob asked.

"An Irish Wolfhound and wolf mix," Zane replied. "Lycos's female wolf went into heat while they were moving. Bethanie didn't know it and took Lady for a walk around the rest area where they'd stopped. Dog was waiting for Lycos to get him out of his crate. The wolfhound was on Lady in a heartbeat. Now Lycos has two pups."

"One is ours," Jewell interjected. She didn't want anyone to stake a claim to the dog.

"Who has the other?" Joseph asked.

"Ethan," Jewell said. "He said Frank about swallowed his taffy when he told him what type of dog it was, but Frank agreed to let Ethan have a wolf on the ranch until his node is ready."

"Speaking of which, how's your setup? Since we're fashioning all the nodes after your system anyway." When Jason's voice came from the video lineup, Jewell clicked on his image to put him on the screen.

"I love it. Ethan is literally in my ear if I need help. The coms are stupendously good. It'll be like heaven when we get the three other modules up."

"Our new people are ready?" Jason asked. As CEO, he kept his fingers in everything.

"We're getting them through the wickets. There aren't any red flags yet." Jewell had acquired new talent, a few fellow hackers she'd worked with over the years. Con, Brando, and Ring's skills were phenomenal, but they had to pass clearance protocols and mental evaluations. It wasn't easy to be hired to work for Guardian, even if you filtered over from the NSA, Department of Defense, or a Fortune 500 company. Even more so since the Siege. "I talked with Honor Buchanan a few minutes ago."

"Your night supervisor?" Jared's voice from the stream pulled her attention down. She added him, Jade, and Nic from a different stream. "Yes. She needs some help." Everyone lifted their heads and stared at her. "I think the incident was hard on her. She's drinking. Pretty heavily. She said she couldn't sleep. I'm worried about her."

"Is she a security risk?" The immediate question popped from Jason.

Jewell shook her head. "No. She doesn't have any of the information she'd need to be a risk. We've reconfigured, rerouted, and enabled new security protocols. Basically, we changed everything. Without me providing access, our system is impenetrable. She's like anyone else who would want to gain access. We've closed it down. It isn't going to happen."

"Where is she?"

"Dallas. I really think she needs professional help." Jewell stared at the screen.

Jason looked up. "What's Wheeler's caseload?"

"I don't have access to that," Jewell said, then looked at Zane. "Am I supposed to?"

"No," Jason answered. "That was a rhetorical question. Get him on the line if you can?"

Jewell popped up and headed to her office. "On it."

"Where are Smoke and Charley?" Anubis asked from the feed.

Jewell called from the office when she heard Anubis' voice say, "Add him, will you?"

"On it," Zane said from the other room.

"A very rare day off for the both of them," Jason said.

Jewell called the number in South Dakota, and Jeremiah Wheeler answered on the third ring. "Dr. Wheeler."

"Hey, Jeremiah, it's Jewell. Can I patch you into a conference call?"

"Sure, my next patient isn't for an hour."

"Perfect. Hold on." Jewell made the connection, checked the security, and went back into the video conference room. She picked up her tablet. "He's on the call, and the line is secure."

"Jeremiah, Jason King here, along with Joseph, Jacob, Jade, Jared, Nic, Kaden, Jewell, and Zane."

"Hey, everyone. To what do I owe this pleasure?" Jeremiah asked.

"We have a computer operator who needs help," Jewell interjected before Jason could say a word.

Zane reached over and placed his hand on hers. "Babe, that's Jason's responsibility."

"Oh. Right. Sorry. I got excited." Jewell pulled her knees up to her chest and stared at the screen in front of her.

"No worries. As Jewell said, one of our primary computer operators seems to have developed a drinking problem since the Siege." Jason put his elbows on the desk in front of him. "I understand what addiction is, and if this incident has pushed Honor over the edge, we owe it to her to get her the help to find her sobriety."

Jeremiah cleared his throat. "She's got to drive this train. No one can make her stop drinking."

Jewell jerked and dropped her legs to the floor. "But she needs help."

"I didn't say I wouldn't try to help her. I said she'd be driving the train." Jeremiah spoke in a caring voice, softening the reprimand. "I have experience with people who fight addictions. And I have space at the moment. I'm releasing one of yours back to duty this week."

"Sage?" Joseph interrupted, and Anubis jerked his head up.

"Yes. He's ready to go back to work," Jeremiah confirmed.

"But back to Honor," Jewell redirected the conversation. "Can we have someone go get her?"

"Jared, what's the manning situation in Dom Ops?"

"Where?" Jared asked as he tapped on his tablet.

"Dallas." Jewell filled in the location.

Jared screwed up his face and shook his head. "I can send someone to check on her, but I'm undermanned in the south. I can't give up a man to babysit. Jacob, do you have a team on tactical rest in the area?"

"A team to pick up one computer programmer

drinking a bit too much. That's overkill, isn't it?" Jade said.

"Probably." Jewell slumped back into her chair.

"Why not Sage?" Jeremiah suggested. "He's not been assigned yet, he's available, and I'd like him to get his feet wet, not be thrown into the deepest depths of the ocean for his first assignment."

"I wouldn't throw him into the ocean. You, that's another story." Joseph's growling response earned him an earful of laughter.

Jeremiah sighed. "I don't doubt it for a minute. Should I remind you once again that I'm happily married with a family?"

"I recall you kissed my wife."

Jeremiah groaned audibly. "*Years* ago. A peck on the lips. You're too protective."

"Being too protective isn't possible," Jason interjected.

"He's right." Zane, Nic, Jared, Anubis, and Jacob seemed to agree at the same time.

"Oh, caveman. Sexy." Jade leaned over and kissed her husband.

"Mind bleach." Jason gruffed as he took off his glasses and rubbed the bridge of his nose. "Okay, it's settled. Doc, tell Sage to call in. Joseph or Anubis, I don't care who, get the details from

Jewell and fill him in. Sorry for interrupting your day, Jeremiah."

"Glad I could help. When you have that lady in hand, I'd be willing to work with her, either here or via video."

"Perfect," Jewell said before the line went dead. Then she made sure the call had disconnected and the conference was still secure. "We're good."

"Okay, on to the staff meeting ..." Jason put his glasses back on and picked up his tablet.

3

Sage Browning slowed as he turned off the highway into Hollister. He'd been staying in a small cabin at the edge of town as he worked with the professionals Guardian had brought in to help him with his stuttering. He smiled ruefully. Doc Wheeler, or Jeremiah as he'd asked Sage to call him, had also worked on his brain a bit. The doctor helped Sage rewire some ways of thinking and such. Sage knew he had baggage, but just how much he was carrying around and why he was hefting the load was illuminating.

Sage full-out smiled at that thought. Look at him go. Illuminating. He said the word out loud, albeit slowly. And he could say any other word he wanted to say. He pulled up in front of the diner. He'd left the Marshall ranch before lunch was served, preferring to grab one of Ciera or Gen's lunch specials before meeting with Jeremiah.

He'd been through so many damn diagnostic tests at the beginning of his stay that he knew just how those lab rats felt, but finally, they had a diagnosis of why he was stuttering. He put the truck into Park in front of the diner and leaned back, staring out the windshield without seeing much of anything. He'd been diagnosed with a psychogenic speech disorder. Which was a long way to say that a psychological process problem caused his stuttering. A mental problem. When they told him that, he landed in an emotional dumpster fire. After spending almost two years watching his momma lose her fight to live and Gus dwindle into a vegetable, he didn't doubt he'd landed one or two issues. Having it confirmed sucked.

But Jeremiah explained it to him, and together with two different speech pathologists and some really neat electronic devices, he had overcome most of his problems. It hadn't been easy, but he went all in and worked hard even when it seemed like the things they were asking him to do were stupid.

"You going to go in, or are you going to continue daydreaming?" Ken Zorn asked from the slatted boardwalk in front of Gen's diner.

Sage smiled and opened his truck's door. He left the keys in the ignition, something his hometown of Bienvenu and Hollister had in common. There weren't any thieves around. Everyone knew everything that happened and who did what to whom. "Ken, how are you?" His speech was slower than everyone else's, or so it seemed to him, but no one mentioned it.

"Having a damn good day. Caught some yahoo from Colorado going over a hundred miles an hour on the highway this morning. Reckless driving and drunk to boot. I called down to Belle, and we got him stopped. You should have seen how pissed that guy was that he ran over that spike strip. He ended up taking a swing at one of the Butte County deputies. They were happy to take the paperwork on for the asshole. I wrote up my statement and headed back up here."

Sage opened the diner door, and they stepped in. "Hey, Ken, Sage," Zeke Johnson said from his corner table. His wife Stephanie sat beside him. "Come sit with us." Zeke motioned to the vacant bench seat. Sage glanced around, noting that almost all the other seats were taken. He nodded and headed over with Ken behind him. "Smells good. What's cooking?" Sage asked as he slid into the booth.

"Pot roast, mashed potatoes, roasted carrots, and apple crumble."

"Ah, Corry's cooking," Ken said as he slid into the seat.

"Yep." Stephanie smiled. "I saw you flying like a bat out of hell past the turn-off this morning, Ken. Everything okay?"

"It is. I was telling Sage about some idiot." Ken launched into the explanation again as Sage glanced around the diner. The small town was so similar to Bienvenu, Louisiana. He needed to stop by and see Beau and Evangeline before too long. He called Beau about once a month and Smoke about once a week. Lord, that assassin would be in his face wanting an update if he didn't. He was a hell of a friend. One of the best people on the planet. It was nice. Having people in your corner. Guardian had made all that possible.

Sage watched as Clay Thompson walked out of the kitchen and headed their way. The kid was working two jobs. Barback at the Bit and Spur on Friday and Saturday nights and bussing tables at the diner during the week. He was a good kid. A hard worker, and Sage enjoyed his company Sunday nights playing cards with him, his dad Mitch, and his Grampa Chester. They'd both been living in the small cottages for about the same amount of time. Sage was supposed to be temporary, whereas the Thompsons seemed to be settling well in the community.

He shook Clay's hand as he passed by, ordered his lunch, and enjoyed the easy comradery. When he was done, he glanced at his watch and excused himself. He laid down a ten-dollar bill and the tip, then headed out into the summer heat. Not that heat in South Dakota was as oppressive as in Plaquemines Parish. No, if you splashed a bucket or three of water on yourself and stood in the midday sun, you might get an idea of the humidity where he'd grown up.

He wandered across the street and waved at Allison, who was behind the counter at the small general store. Her momma was making bread, and the delicious aroma hung in the air. It was damn good sourdough. After his weekly chat with Jeremiah, he'd pick up a loaf on the way back to his truck.

He strolled down the boardwalk and trudged

through the dirt between the buildings before hopping back on the boardwalk in front of Jeremiah's building. The little town was in a growing phase, and several buildings were in the process of being built or remodeled. It was good to see the town thriving.

Going around to the back entrance, he opened the door to see Jeremiah standing at the counter reading a medical file. He glanced up. "Right on time."

Sage glanced at his watch. "I'm fifteen minutes early."

"Which, for you, is right on time." Jeremiah smiled. "Come on in."

Sage followed Jeremiah to his office and dropped into the comfy leather chair he always sat in. Jeremiah sat across from him.

"So, how was last week?"

"No problems. No, that's not true. I had a rough time with the word triangle for some reason."

"Some reason?" Jeremiah leaned back.

Sage chuckled. "I was trying to figure out a cut on one of the pieces of lumber on a project. I'm helping one of the foster kid's out at Drake's build. I needed it to be an exact match for the one already in place. I suck at math, and I screwed up the cut. *Twice*. I couldn't reach the triangle and asked Ben to pass it to me. The entire sentence was a hard hit. I mean, it was like I was transported back in time to when I first showed up. As soon as I realized what I was doing, I used the methods I'd learned. But it was a reminder that I'm a work in progress."

"There are triggers for you." Jeremiah nodded.

"I know, and I accept that," Sage agreed, thinking back through the devices and exercises he'd used to overcome his stuttering. For him, the best electronic devices in the world were earpieces that echoed his voice into his ears, so it sounded like someone else was talking with him. He could talk without stuttering as long as he had that voice speaking at the same time he was. After years of frustration and thinking, as the military said, a brain injury caused a permanent stutter, the ease of speaking while using that equipment had brought tears to his eyes. And he didn't give a flying fuck who saw him break down.

"I talked with Guardian this morning."

Sage blinked and looked at Jeremiah. "About?"

"You. You don't need to be here any longer. We can talk through what we have remaining via video conference."

"Yeah?" Sage leaned forward and smiled. "I'm going to go back to work?"

Jeremiah tipped his head from side to side. "Well, kind of."

That didn't sound good. "Care to explain?"

Jeremiah put the tablet he was holding down. "I don't have all the details, but I suggested you for a job the staff had problems finding someone to handle. I'm sure you'll get a better brief when you call in, which they want you to do as soon as we're done. From what I gathered, a computer programmer is having an issue and needs someone to get her and bring her in for some help."

"A babysitter." Sage narrowed his eyes at Jeremiah. "Why would you recommend me for that type of job?"

"Because I didn't want you thrown into the deep end of the pool right off the bat, and with Guardian's rebuild, I had no doubt that could happen."

Sage's gut dropped. "You don't think I could handle it? Being thrown into the deep end."

"I don't doubt you *could* handle it. I just didn't want you to *have* to handle it if you know what I mean."

Sage shook his head. Those points didn't cross in his book. Jeremiah would have to explain it to him. "No. Can't say as I do."

"It's been a while since you worked as a Guardian."

Sage leaned back in his chair. Oh. Man, didn't the doc know how ingrained the military and Guardian were to him? "I've gone through the most advanced training offered at the Rose, and for the time I've been working with you, I've been doing physical conditioning and weapons qualifications at the ranch. Plus, while I've been twiddling my fingers here, I've taken courses from the Rose via secure video. My ability *hasn't* diminished." Just the fucking opposite.

"But your reaction time may have. Stepping back in slowly isn't a mark against you, Sage."

Sage held up a hand and shook his head. "Doc, you've never been in my field of work. How would you know if it is or isn't a mark against me?"

Jeremiah stared at him for a moment. "Checkmate. You are correct. I don't know that it isn't a mark against you, but I'll make sure it won't be."

Sage shook his head. "No offense, but leave it. I'll grab this lady programmer and take her wherever she needs to go." Sage stood up. He was cleared for duty. Well, somewhat cleared. Regard-less, it was a good feeling. He extended his hand. "Thank you for everything, Jeremiah. I don't know how to tell you how much you've helped."

"You just did, Sage." Jeremiah stood up and clasped Sage's hand, pulling him in for a quick bro hug. "Video conference after this babysitting trip. Just call and set up an appointment."

"Got it." Sage lifted his hand as he walked out of the office. He wouldn't blow off Jeremiah; he still had work to do on himself and would make sure he finished what he'd started.

Sage pulled up outside of his little cottage and headed inside, taking two steps at a time up the front steps. Inside, he sat down on the couch and drew a deep breath before he called in.

"Operator Two Seven Four. How may I direct your call?

"This is Sage Browning calling for Fury or Anubis." He smiled as he spoke.

"Welcome back. Please hold while I connect you." He pulled the phone away from his ear. He never thought he'd say it, but he missed that AI operator.

"Well, it's about damn time." Fury's voice grated over the line.

"Missed you, too."

"Bet you did," Fury snipped. "In order to spring you from that evil doctor's hands, I had to agree to let you go on a retrieval mission. I've sent the dossier to the Ranch. Chief will give it to you. Are you armed?"

"I have my personal weapon."

"Vehicle?"

"Also my personal vehicle."

"Okay. We've got a couple of travel kits at the Ranch. I'll have Chief pull one out and check it over. You'll take it with you, just in case."

A travel kit, also known as a mini arsenal. "Where am I going?"

"Dallas. Not sure what's up with this chick, but use your best judgment. You don't have a call sign since you and Smoke split up." Joseph sighed. "The Thorn teams have been disbanded. Use Thorn One. I'll let everyone know. I need you to head out tomorrow morning. As far as we know, this isn't urgent, so you don't have to bust your ass getting there. Let me know your ETA, and I'll let the people monitoring her know."

Sage frowned. God, he missed being with Smoke on the Thorn teams. They'd worked some missions that would never see the light of day. An assassin and a tactical specialist sent in to do things normal five men teams couldn't do. But it was over, and he was moving on. He wondered, "She's one of our programmers, right?"

"Yep. I understand she was in the building when it exploded. She was one of the lucky few who got out. From what I can tell, she's been hiding in a bottle since then."

"Damn. Tough."

"Everyone handles shit in different ways."

"Don't I know it." Sage snorted.

"By the way. It's good to talk with you. Looking forward to you getting your ass back to work."

"Not any more than I am. Any idea what I'll be doing?"

"I've got an idea, but we haven't fine-tuned the concept. You'll be busy, but that's not a bad thing." Fury chuckled. "You've had enough time on your ass."

"Looking forward to getting back in the mix of things." Sage glanced at his watch. He needed to get back to the ranch, pick up that kit, then clean out the cottage. Not that he had much there. He'd give what he did pick up over the time he'd been there to the Thompsons next door.

"Good to know. Call in when you know your ETA. Whatever it takes."

"As long as it takes." Sage smiled as he disconnected the call. It was the first time he'd said those words in one hell of a long time.

4

Honor tripped over an empty bottle of vodka as she held onto the wall and made her way to the kitchen. She gagged a bit, and the bile that bubbled up from her stomach burned the back of her throat. God, her mouth tasted like a cesspool. She hit the light switch, but nothing happened. Even after flicking it off and back on again, darkness still reigned. "What the hell?"

She dropped against the wall and pushed her hair out of her face. Her fingers caught in the snarls and knots. Honor looked around and glanced down at the pile of mail on the floor. Fuck. Red overdue stamps glared at her from the tile. She'd forgotten to pay the utility bill. What day was it? What was the time? Where was her phone?

Pushing herself off the wall, she finished her trek into the kitchen and turned on the water, cupping handfuls to her mouth, not caring to find a clean cup. She turned off the water and dried her hands on her jeans as she walked back to the small living room.

Moving the empty bottles from around the couch where she'd fallen asleep, she found her phone and hit the face. Damn it. Saturday. She leaned against the back of the couch. That meant at least two days without power before she could pay her bill on Monday.

Her head ached, and she rubbed her temples. She needed a drink. Grabbing bottles off the floor, she searched for one with liquor. She found one with about an inch of vodka left in the bottom. It took thirty seconds to down the small amount. Honor rubbed her face and looked at her phone again. Seven. She glanced at the window above her. The yellow hue gave her no clue if it was morning or night. It didn't matter. She needed a drink. Honor grabbed what was left of her cash and shoved it into her pocket. After slipping on a pair of tennis shoes, she grabbed her phone and pushed herself up, making her way to the front door.

Between her place and the liquor store were two bars. One was a biker hangout. She walked past that one even though it was the quickest way to a drink. The men used to make catcalls at her. Used to. Now they just watched her stagger by. Whatever. She still didn't like the place. She stumbled and grabbed onto the rails of the stairs down to the Tube, a dive bar a block up. She found an empty bar stool and placed a hundred-dollar bill on the bar. "Vodka and keep them coming until that runs out."

The bartender took the money and held it up to the light before he marked it with a marker to see if it was counterfeit. Honor watched him place the bill on the back shelf and pour her a shot of vodka. She held up her hand, stopping him from leaving. Downing the shot, she motioned for him to pour another and then a third. He refilled her and lifted an eyebrow. Whatever. She talked to the man without looking at him. "You got food here?"

"Yeah. You want a menu?"

She shook her head. "Hamburger or whatever."

The bartender put the vodka bottle back on the

shelf and made his way to the kitchen. Honor hooked her feet around the bar stool and blinked at the television. She watched as the weatherman drew large circles around areas of blue ocean. He swept his arm toward Mexico and the Gulf while using his hand to indicate where the storm could go. Little lines in different colors spanned the entire map. Yeah, no one had a clue. "Big storm," she muttered.

She stared at her glass and noticed her fingernails. They were broken and chipped. A line of dirt delineated her nail from the bed. She lifted her fingers and examined them. "Damn." She lifted her other hand and stared at those nails, muttering out loud. Her hands shook as the image of her dirty fingernails worked its way through the vodka in her system. The side of her hand was covered in dirt. She turned her hands and stared at the palms. Oh, God. She turned her hands over. Where was her ring? Her mother's wedding ring? It was all she had left of her mom. Honor patted the pockets of her jeans and pulled out the cash, frantically sorting through it.

No, no, no! "What have you done?" She looked up into the mirror behind the bar. The woman who stared back at her was unrecognizable. She stared at the rat's nest her hair had become, then glanced down at her shirt. The stained, crumpled material looked as if it had been buried and then dug up. She lifted her eyes to the mirror again, and her hands covered her mouth as she realized how far she'd fallen. "Oh, God. I need help."

Jewell. She pulled out her phone and stared at the incoming call log. Two days ago. Fuck. She'd lost two days. She hit the number and put the phone to her ear. "Are you okay?" Jewell asked immediately.

"No. I lost it. It's not here." Tears welled in her eyes.

"What did you lose?"

"Momma's ring. Oh, God, Jewell. I need help. I need ..." She swiped a tear. "I can't do this anymore."

"I've got someone coming to get you. His name is Sage, and he's already in Dallas. Where are you right now? You're not at home."

"I'm at the Tube." Honor grabbed a cocktail napkin and knocked over her vodka. "Shit."

"Honor. I want you to stay there, okay?"

A hamburger and fries appeared in front of her. Her stomach flipped, and bile rose in her throat. She pushed the food away. "How long?"

"He'll be there soon. Just wait right there."

"No. I have to find my ring." Honor hung up and put the phone on the bar.

"One for the road?" The bartender picked up her glass and wiped away the spilled vodka with a bar towel.

Honor stared at the glass. The overwhelming desire to numb the feelings of loss, disgust, and helplessness roared over her, cloaking her in a raging need for the nothingness the alcohol provided. She licked her lips, staring at the bottle in the man's hand. He started to pour the liquor, but she shook her head. "No." The word croaked from her throat as she grabbed her phone and slid off the barstool, catching herself as she landed on the floor.

"Hey, you left money here. Yo, lady!" the bartender called.

Honor let the door slam behind her and climbed the stairs to the street, heading back the way she'd come. She wrapped her arms around herself, cold even on the hot August evening.

"Hey, you keep walking by here. You need something?"

Honor looked up. A fat biker wearing jeans and a leather vest called to her from the corner of the bar and cupped his crotch. "No." She shrunk in on herself and tried to hurry past him, but the biker snagged her arm in his grip. Honor pulled away. "Let me go!"

Someone laughed. "She's gross, man. You don't want to tap that. You'll catch a disease."

Another voice chided, "Man, you aren't that desperate, are you?"

Honor fought, pulling away from the biker that had her in his grip. "Let me go! Stop. Help! Somebody! Help!"

His big hand covered her mouth and nose. Honor tried to scream, but the hand clamped down harder, clogging her ability to breathe. Honor struggled. Her desperation for air became as strong as her fear of the man holding her. The edges of her vision started to darken. She heard a shout before the darkness enveloped her.

"Sage, you need to hurry."

"What's going on?" Sage turned the corner, pulling up in front of the address he'd been given.

Jewell answered, "She's at a bar, and she's ... I don't know. Something's wrong."

"Address?"

"Sending it now." Sage tapped on the address and hit directions on his maps app. He put the vehicle into park. "Three minutes." He slammed the truck back into gear, ran a red light, and floored the gas. "Picture?"

"On your phone." He hit the screen when he was forced to stop at a red light. A picture popped onto his phone. *Damn.*

"This is a screen capture from three days ago when I talked to her."

The woman looked like hell, but Sage committed the picture to memory. He pulled through the intersection and looked right. "*Aw, shit.*"

"What? What's happening?" Jewell asked frantically.

Sage swerved to the right, almost taking out another truck before slamming on the brakes. His truck hit the curb and jumped it, landing on the sidewalk. He jammed the truck into Park before getting out and bellowing, "Hey!" Sage moved toward the fat biker who had Honor. The man sneered and let her go, dropping her to the sidewalk. She fell like a dead weight.

Sage saw the other two motorheads move to

flank him. *Bring it on motherfuckers.* "If she's hurt, you're dead."

The man who had Honor reached out with a massive boot and flopped her out of his way. "You got a death wish, boy?" The man walked toward him as the others moved with him.

Not a time for words. Sage advanced quickly and throat-punched the son of a bitch. He swung around and ducked a slow and poorly aimed fist from the man on his right flank. Sage powered through with an uppercut to the man's gut. He felt two meat hooks grab his biceps, pinning his arms to his side. Sage leaned down and reared back as hard as he could. The crack of his head against the man's nose loosened the grip immediately. The one who'd had Honor was still on the ground, choking and turning a deep shade of red. His two other attackers kept their distance.

"Call an ambulance." *If you want that fucker to live.* Sage said as he picked up Honor and tossed her over his shoulder. He drew his weapon from his shoulder. The forty-five-caliber lifted as a covey of men busted out of the bar entrance.

Sage swung the gun to the lead man, moving toward his truck as he spoke. "They started it. I finished it."

Hands went up in the air. The man leading the charge out of the bar looked around. "Ah, fuck. Man, we don't ride with these guys, but be warned, they have friends with bad attitudes. Everyone, get back inside the bar. Not our fight."

Sage held the gun on the crowd until they were inside, and he heard a siren's wail getting closer. He managed to open the passenger door and flop Honor onto the seat while still holding the gun on the three original attackers. Then he made his way to the driver's side door and got in. He was out of there two seconds later.

"What's going on?" Zane's voice demanded an answer.

"She was in trouble." Sage pulled around the corner, reaching for Honor as he spoke. He found her neck under the tangle of hair and sighed with relief when he found a pulse. "She's alive. Bikers had her cornered."

"Damn it," Zane swore before commanding, "Get her out of that town."

"No," Jewell said emphatically. "Wait, you have to go back to her house. Her computers. Don't leave without them."

Sage shook his head. *Computers can be replaced.*

"Zane, please," Jewell pleaded.

Bengal sighed. "Go back to the apartment."

"The police. I might have killed one of them," Sage said but hit the blinker to turn right. "Throat punch."

"I'll have someone handle that," Zane said. "She's a programmer, dude. Those computers are essential."

"Machines," Sage mumbled as he turned the corner again. He could see DPD patrol cars in front of the biker bar as he parked. An ambulance whizzed by him as he turned off his truck in front of Honor's building. Honor jerked and gasped, careening off the seat toward the floor before pushing herself up and grabbing her head. She looked around, saw him, and slammed backward, grabbing at the door handle.

Sage held up his hand. "I'm Guardian."

"He's with us. This is Sage. I told you he was coming to help you," Jewell confirmed from the speakerphone.

The woman glanced toward the bar. "He was going to rape me."

Sage backed up a bit. The woman's breath reeked, but he tried not to let her see his reaction. They needed to get the computers and get out of dodge. "You don't have to worry about him anymore. You're safe." Sage turned off the vehicle, grabbed his phone, and got out of his truck. Walking around, he caught Honor as she almost fell from the vehicle. "Where's your apartment?"

She pointed down the stairs. Sage walked beside her as she pushed through several garbage bags placed around dumpsters outside her door. She turned the handle and walked inside.

"You didn't lock the door?"

"I don't know." The woman's despondency was at odds with the quick and alert way she'd woken up. He stared at her and then past her for several seconds before he realized what he was looking at. *Shit.* "Place is trashed."

"Someone broke in?" Jewell said from the phone.

Sage nodded even though they couldn't see him. "Think so."

"No one broke in," Honor grumped before moving into the kitchen and lifting empty bottles.

God, the place was a mess. Sage moved to a clear spot on the linoleum flooring and watched as the woman moved crap around. "What are you looking for?"

"My ring."

Sage watched her move bottles and trash around. "What kind of ring?"

"A wedding ring. Gold with three diamonds." She kept moving trash and bottles.

He glanced around him and listened to yet another siren warble by. *Man, we need to get gone.* Sage walked out of the kitchen and into the living room. Good God, by the number of empty vodka bottles in the house, he'd be surprised if the woman had a liver left. He flipped the switch to turn on the light. "Power is out."

"I didn't pay the bill." The response came from the kitchen in between clunks, clanks, and tinkling noises. "It's not here."

"I can fix the power issue," Jewell said.

Sage looked at the phone and then at the mess. There were two laptops on the coffee table among a collection of bottles. "Are these your computers?"

"Two of them." Honor's voice came from behind him.

He twisted around to see her in the dimness of the front room. "There are more?"

"One." She moved to the closet and opened it. Pointing to the ceiling, she said, "My primary is up there. I'll get a chair." It was then he realized how small she was. He was six feet two inches tall. She couldn't be much over five feet. As he looked down, the anger and anxiety drained, and a need to protect her rushed through him. She seemed so slight and vulnerable, more like a bird ravaged by a storm than a person. Someone needed to shield her from harm until she found whatever she was searching for at the bottom of the bottle.

Shaking off the thought, Sage moved over, making out a small hole in the ceiling at the top of the wall. "Let me see if I can get it." He stood on his toes and could just finger the computer to the side and then was able to grab it. He put the ... box— because it wasn't a laptop—beside the other two computers. "Is there anything else?"

"Like what?" Honor turned around and looked at the cube on the table.

"A computer?" He pointed to the other laptops.

"No, *that's* all three of my computers."

Sage frowned at the small cube. "A metal box?"

"Computers don't have to have a monitor." Jewell chuckled.

"In my world, they do," Zane said.

"Amen," Sage agreed.

Honor started moving bottles around again. Sage wanted to get the hell out of the apartment. It stunk, was filled with empty liquor bottles, and

God only knew how many cockroaches were lurking under the pizza boxes and take-out wrappers that littered the floor.

He couldn't believe that someone could ignore the decline of a loved one, leaving her to hit rock bottom and do nothing to prevent it. How could a man worth his salt leave his wife to struggle like that? Why she cherished a ring given to her by someone who deserted her was beyond him. "Look, I'm sure your husband will understand."

"What?" The woman stood up slowly and stared at him like he'd spoken Greek or something. Sage stopped. Full stop, as in froze. Had he stuttered? No, not once during the entire event, which had been about as stressful as it could get. He held on to that nugget of information. Fuck, that emergency pick-up was a middle-of-the-pool dousing, not quite the deep end that Jeremiah was talking about. But he hadn't stuttered. Wait until he told Jeremiah. *Fuck yes.* He did an internal fist pump, totally hyped at the revelation.

The lights blinked on. "Power's on," Sage acknowledged for Jewell, who he knew was still listening.

"DPD is taken care of. No need to worry. All three declined medical treatment, couldn't describe the assailant, and there were no witnesses inside the bar," Zane said.

"Copy." Well, that was a damn good thing because they wouldn't have had to look far. He was literally a block from the bar where the DPD was congregating.

Honor moved more bottles around. The stink of old alcohol in the apartment was overpowering. Sage moved to the AC unit and tried to turn it on.

"It's broken," Honor said from where she was on the floor, looking under the couch without a flashlight.

"Great." He went to the high windows and used the crank to open them. Any fresh air in the place would be a help. He watched her as she moved shit from one place to the other. "Look, possessions can be replaced."

"Not this. This is my mom's ring. It's all I have left of her. I have to find the ring." The woman muttered as she continued to move shit.

"When was the last time you remember having it?" Sage toed a pizza box. A cockroach, the size of South Dakota, scurried from under it. Sage stomped on the fucker and shivered. He hated roaches. They had them in Louisiana, too. That was why he was raised being meticulous about being clean. The fuckers thrived on pieces of food, bits of this and that. His family didn't have the money for an exterminator to visit every quarter, so they kept the bugs manageable by ensuring nothing was left out to attract them.

"What's going on?" Zane asked.

Sage told him what he knew. "She's looking for a ring."

Honor stood up. In her hand was a bottle about half full. Sage moved over and reached for it, but she jerked it away, keeping it away from him. Then she walked into the kitchen, and Sage followed her. Standing in front of the sink, Sage wagered it was a fifty-fifty shot whether or not the lady would chug the vodka or pour it out. He waited quietly as Honor faced her battle. He'd lived his entire life with a mean alcoholic. He couldn't help her make this decision.

It took several minutes, but the woman slowly tipped the bottle and poured the alcohol down the drain. He watched, feeling a mix of emotions swirling. He was proud of her for taking this first step toward sobriety. Though he knew every moment going forward would be hard, she had gripped the courage to empty that bottle. Whether she realized it in her state or not, she'd begun the process of changing her life in one single act. Her hands shook slightly as she placed the bottle on the countertop with a gentle thud—an unmistakable acknowledgment that something monumental had just happened. Sage wanted to cheer but remained quiet. It was her victory.

She stared at the empty bottle and said, "In the bedroom."

"What?" Sage had no idea what the woman was talking about.

"The last place I remember having my mother's ring." Honor walked past him, and he turned, following her. She walked through the living room, past a small half-bathroom, and opened the bedroom door.

He stopped at the doorway of a pristinely clean room. *Out of place much?* The closet door was open, and her clothes were hanging neatly. The bed was made, and there was a slight smell of lavender. "Don't use this room?"

Honor walked over to the small nightstand and pulled open the drawer. She reached in and picked up the ring. "It has mirrors."

Sage glanced around. The closet doors were mirrored, and there were two large mirrors on opposite walls. The bathroom door also had a mirror on it. "I don't understand."

She put the ring on her right ring finger and wrapped her arms around herself. "When you hate yourself, looking at your reflection is the last thing you want to do."

Oh, boy. So, yeah, the woman has some hardcore issues. More than simply liking booze too much. "Do you want to shower before we go?"

Honor glanced at the bathroom and then held up her hands, staring at her fingers. He didn't rush her. Instead, he leaned against the door jamb and gave her the time and space she needed. "Do we have the time?"

"Yeah, sure." Sage backed out of the room. "Take your time." He shut the door behind him and stared at the disaster in the living room. He pulled his phone out of his shirt pocket and took it off speaker. Walking to the front door, he opened it and flipped open three of the big green dumpster lids, eyeing the trash bags lying around them. *Empty. Lazy-ass people.*

Sage drew a deep breath and slowly let it out. "She's getting cleaned up. Am I taking her back to South Dakota or a rehab facility?"

"Jewell's making calls now. She's pretty messed up, isn't she?"

"Yeah. That sums it up." Sage glanced back into the apartment.

"Stay with her. We'll figure out the next step."

"That wasn't done before I got here?" Sage picked up two trash bags on the walkway and tossed them into the empty dumpster.

"Dude, this was never a typical pickup. That woman has mad skills on the computer. She was our nighttime supervisor in DC, and she's a personal friend of my wife's. She's not an assignment. She's a friend who doesn't have to return to Guardian or get help. She needs to make that choice for herself."

Sage stood with a hand on his hip and stared into the apartment. "I didn't have to ask for help or come back to Guardian," he spoke to himself, but out loud.

Zane didn't say anything for a moment, then asked, "What made you decide to come back?"

"I made a promise to Smoke." *But I could have backed out of that and kept my ass down in Bienvenu.* Sage had made peace with his momma before she passed, and Gus was in a nursing home and would be until he left the earth. Sage had had his momma's house rebuilt and refurnished while he was up in South Dakota. Beau and Evangeline had checked on the contractor and sent him pictures and videos. He'd also watched the construction from game cameras he'd posted around the property. It was easy to link in and see what the contractor was doing to the outside of his mom's house. Granted, the house was his, but he hadn't decided whether he was selling or keeping it. Yeah, he could have stayed. He knew some assholes, but the good people outweighed the jerks.

"That brought you back. What made you get help?" Zane asked.

Sage took his time answering the question. He was bluntly honest, "I hated the fact that I stuttered. I did research and knew I could get better. I might never be one hundred percent, but I could improve."

"I haven't heard you stutter all day," Zane said.

"I still have my moments. When I get upset or frustrated, I do. I guess I didn't have time to be either earlier today." Sage was still amazed and couldn't wait to talk with Jeremiah.

Zane was quiet for a moment, then cleared his throat. "You've been with Honor. What do you think she needs?"

Sage rubbed the back of his neck. "I'd want a place to dry out and figure out what to do next. Somewhere safe."

Zane made a noise of agreement. "Do you happen to know of anywhere within driving distance?"

Sage's mind instantly slid to Bienvenu. It was close enough to drive through the night and be there for breakfast. He shook his head. "No, I don't."

Zane huffed. "Yes, you do. Can you think of a better place to take her?"

"Hollister." Sage's answer was immediate.

"How do you think she'd fare on a two-day road trip?" Zane's question brought up memories of Gus trying to quit drinking cold turkey when he and his brothers were growing up. Those days were hell, not only for Gus, who went through sweats and vomiting, but for the rest of his family because being sick made Gus meaner. Of course, Gus was a lifetime drunk. He didn't think Honor was. Still, a road trip that long wouldn't be pleasant for anyone. "Damn hard. A rehab facility?"

"We still have to find one with room for her and get her to agree to go. I'm looking for a temporary place where she'll be safe, looked after, and can start pulling her shit together."

Well, Bienvenu is that, Sage mentally admitted. "Rehab is best. I can't force her to go."

"I'll have Jewell talk to her."

"Yeah, give her thirty minutes or so. I think she needs some time alone right now," Sage spoke slowly.

"I'll hang up. Give me a ring if she's ready to leave before Jewell can find a facility." Bengal wound up the call.

"Can do." He hung up and stared at the mess. He knew rehab was what the woman needed. Jewell would have more luck than him on that topic. But if she didn't, Bienvenu was a place Honor could heal without judgment or stigma. He had friends there, and it was isolated. A perfect place where she could start fresh and have every opportunity to get back on track with life. But he wasn't the one to make that decision. He stared at the mess and started picking up bottles. It was entirely possible he'd fill all the empty trash bins before he was done with the front room.

5

Honor sat on the small bench in the shower letting the water pour over her knees and feet. She'd washed and rewashed, scrubbing the filth she felt but couldn't see. She washed her hair three times and let the conditioner sit in it before trying to drag a comb through to get rid of the knots. Her hands were shaking, and she wanted a drink. God, she wanted a drink. Her stomach ached, and her head hurt. She reached up and rubbed the egg on the back of her head, wincing. She didn't know how she'd gotten it.

Glancing down at her mom's wedding band, the desire for a drink didn't lessen. It was still there. She couldn't deny it, but she'd been so drunk that she thought she'd lost her mom's ring. She'd been so drunk she didn't remember the two days between talking to Jewell and today. *What had she done? Had she gone out for more alcohol?* She dropped her head into her hands. Had she gone on the computer? She didn't know. Had she given away her location? The thought sent chills through her. Her teeth chattered. She moved her legs and turned off the spray when the water ran cold. She'd wait ten minutes and turn it back on.

Out of routine, she reached for the wide tooth comb and started to work it through her hair. With each pull, she tugged up unwanted memories. Dean's face flashed through her thoughts. He'd played her and used her. She gritted her teeth and started rocking back and forth, her hair forgotten. If she'd only seen through his act, everyone would still be alive.

Honor opened her eyes and closed them again as her stomach lurched. She leaned against the shower wall, shivering.

A knock on the door proceeded, "Everything all right?"

Honor sat up. "Yeah, I'm waiting for the water to warm up again."

"All right." The man, what was his name? She couldn't remember. He was from Guardian. She relaxed a bit. Jewell had sent him. Sent him to bring her back to Guardian.

Could she return and not see ghosts of the people who should still be alive? She picked up her comb, worked it through a lock that had been detangled, and started on the next piece of hair. The repeated short strokes, gradually working out the snarls, gave her something to concentrate on, but her memories still flashed back all those years ago. To Dean.

Honor stopped in shock as her boyfriend looked up from her laptop. "Why are you on my computer?"

"I needed something, and I got it." The man pulled a thumb drive out of her PC.

"What?" She rushed into her living room. She'd been at work. Newly hired at Guardian Security, she'd volunteered to work late on a special project. She'd told Dean she'd be home later than she was but happily came home earlier than anticipated. She didn't expect to see him on her computer.

Dean brushed off her concern. "Relax, babe. I took the Nutcracker program."

Honor lunged toward him, grabbing for the jump drive in his hand. "No. Give that back to me. That program is dangerous if the wrong people use it." She'd worked damn hard on the project and knew that given the right amount of computer power and operator skill, it could drill through any firewall. If it fell into the wrong hands, the person who used it could cause untold problems.

Dean lifted it over his head and laughed. "What are you going to do? Tell Guardian you gave me a program that could hack into the Department of Defense? A program you wrote for me because you wanted me to love you."

"What? What does that mean? I didn't give it to you. You're stealing it!" She jumped up, trying to reach the drive.

"Bullshit. You gave me the password to your computer. You gave me access to your apartment. You told me all about the program. Hell, you stupid bitch, you developed it because I bet you that you couldn't. You made this program for me, and I'm taking it." He shoved her, sending her flying onto the couch. "If you tell anyone I have it, I'll bring you down with me. You'll go to jail before I will. I have plenty of friends who will testify exactly what I tell them to say."

She clutched her stomach. "You can't. Oh, my God, Dean, why ... what ... Why would you do this to me?

You said you loved me." She stood up and tried to get the drive again.

"*God, I'm so sick of your whining. Love you? Not in a million years. I forced myself to dip my dick into you. I forced myself to get and stay hard. Fuck, I had to think of actual women to get off. You're fat, you're disgusting, and you'll always be alone. I have what I want now, and I'm out of here. Tell a soul, and I'll make sure you go to jail." He slapped her so hard that she spun and fell. The bruise he'd left had healed; the way he'd shattered her heart hadn't.*

Honor drew a deep lungful of air and vomited onto the shower floor. Leaning against the shower wall, she cried silently. Dean had used that program or given it to someone who had. They'd used it to identify the plane on which Archangel and Jason King were flying. They used it to identify Archangel's wife's location and to locate and blow up the trailer where Jason King's fiancée lived. The hacker, a Russian she'd later found out, had moved onto folders that held highly sensitive information. That was when Honor spotted *her* program as it burrowed through Guardian's internal firewalls.

It was a Godsend that she was working the night shift when the attack happened. She'd been waiting to hear about her program, waiting to view the reports about the program that drilled through firewalls, but she hadn't. Not until that night.

Honor had anticipated that moment for the previous two and a half years. She'd built a new program that could defeat the one she'd originally created. She'd been waiting to kill the Nutcracker. That night, while all of Guardian watched the events unfold with the aircraft, the vehicle Archangel's wife was driving, and the explosion in Georgia, she backtracked the program and laid waste to the originating computer. Honor worked feverously to ensure no one ever knew it was her program. The hacker who used it would never use it again. She made sure of it. Honor prayed that was the last she'd ever see of the program or Dean.

Unfortunately, her prayers were unanswered.

Honor leaned forward and turned on the water. She hadn't eaten anything in as long as she could remember. The hot water chased her stomach bile and vodka down the drain. Honor washed again and stood under the hot water to rinse her hair.

She moved slower than normal. Her head ached, and she was so damn cold, plus there was that want, no, the need for a drink. The sensation seemed to jump from one nerve to the next, causing her muscles to twitch and ache. Brushing her teeth was an effort. She was tired, and her body and head hurt, but she managed to finish combing her hair one last time. She noticed the length and sighed. How long had it been since she'd had her hair cut?

She didn't have the energy or will to figure that out. Honor pulled on some underwear and blinked at how her hipbones protruded and the slack in the elastic around her waist. She looked across the room and stared at her body in the mirror. Honor walked closer, not recognizing herself. Gone were the thick thighs that rubbed together when she walked and the bulging muffin top that rounded her waist and ruined every outfit she tried to wear. She could see her ribs. Honor ran a finger over each bump, then dropped her hand. She'd lost a lot of weight. She would have been over the moon happy at any other time in her life. Now, it didn't matter. It didn't matter at all.

Honor pulled on a bra and t-shirt, slid on a pair of jeans, and found a belt. She cinched the belt to the last hole and put on a pair of socks and tennis shoes. She glanced down at her nails. The dirt was gone, but the broken nails still stood as a stark reminder of rock bottom. That was where she saw herself in that bar mirror. The memory of what she looked like then was deeply ingrained. The bar was her rock bottom. It was where she made the call for help. She could never let herself fall back into the hole she'd dug. God help her; if she ever got out, she'd never return.

Honor opened the bedroom door and blinked. The man from Guardian had a mop and a bucket and was scrubbing the floor. His muscles bunched and released under his t-shirt as he worked on the floor at the entryway of her apartment. The bottles and garbage were gone. His black leather jacket and a shoulder holster with a very big gun were placed neatly on a chair she'd forgotten she had. Honor looked around in disbelief. Had she been in the shower that long? Had she blacked out again? She glanced up at the windows. It was dark out. "What time is it?"

The man stopped and turned around, glancing at his watch. "Nine thirty."

She frowned at him. "You're from Guardian?"

"Sage Browning." He leaned against the mop. His long dark hair touched his shoulders. He had a nice smile. Honor rubbed her arms. It was awkward to talk to someone. She hadn't had a casual conversation in months, almost a year, actually. "Jewell has been trying to call you."

Honor jumped a bit when he spoke. "I don't have my phone." She still rubbed her arms, but the movement couldn't warm her. "I might have left it somewhere. Unless you found it."

"No, no phone." He placed the mop into the bucket, reached into his back pocket, and handed her his phone. It was a nice one, one of the latest models. One like she had. Where did she leave it? She stared at the phone without moving. "You can use it." Sage prompted her out of her thoughts.

She reached for it and looked around the apartment. "Thank you."

He shrugged and nodded at the phone. "Call her." He picked up the bucket and mop and went into the kitchen.

Honor glanced around the room. *No!* She ran into the kitchen. "Where are my computers?"

"Locked safely in my truck with my travel kit. They're secure." Sage said, pouring the dirty water down the drain.

"Oh. Okay." She dropped her hands to her knees, still holding his phone, and drew gasping breaths. Her wet hair fell from her back and slapped her in the face.

She heard the bucket clatter into the sink and saw cowboy boots in front of her. "Need help?"

Honor let herself go limp and sat on the floor. Weak, shivering, and cold, she wrapped her arms around her legs and cried.

Somehow, she was wrapped in warm arms and pulled into the man sitting on the floor beside her. The contact made her cry harder. She had no idea how long she cried or how long he held her after she'd stopped. He didn't move, just kept holding her in his arms on the kitchen floor as she slowly pulled herself together.

Honor felt something unfamiliar stirring. A quiet warmth. The embrace was tight enough to sink in, to feel, yet not overwhelming enough to make it strange or uncomfortable. She closed her eyes, realizing that was what kindness felt like. She sighed against him before finally pulling away. Reluctant to break the warmth, she wanted to cling to the moment of compassion. The moment a stranger took the time to sit with her in silence yet say with every fiber of his being that she was safe. Finally, she wiped away the tears and snot. God, she was a disgusting mess. She moved away from him. "I'm sorry."

He didn't say anything. Instead, he picked up his phone, unlocked it, and handed it to her. "Time to call Jewell."

She nodded and watched as he stood up and went to the sink to finish cleaning as if her breakdown hadn't happened.

Honor called the CCS number she knew by heart, and the phone was answered on the first ring. "Is she okay?" Jewell snapped the question.

"I'm not even close to being okay. I don't know what happened to my phone." Honor stared at the pattern stamped into the linoleum flooring.

"Okay. Okay," Jewell said. There was relief in her voice. "We've got a couple of options for what can happen next."

Honor glanced at the cowboy boots as they walked out of the kitchen. "What options?"

"I can send you to a rehab facility. There are several good ones, but we have to wait for an opening. I'm trying to pull in favors to make that happen."

Honor huffed, "I'm not doing drugs."

"Alcohol is an addiction, too," Jewell said emphatically.

"I know that." Honor could feel her mouth water at the thought of a drink. "What other options?"

"There's a doctor in South Dakota. He'll help you get better."

"The Annex?" She'd worked on bringing the Annex online with all the others.

"Yep. Well, the town just north of there."

Hollister. Honor dropped her head to her free hand. "What else?"

"You can stay with Zane and me. We've moved, and there isn't a liquor store within a hundred miles." Jewell chuckled. "We're getting a puppy and everything, with plenty of room."

"Why would you want my problems?"

"Because we're friends," Jewell replied quickly.

Honor traced the pattern of the linoleum and felt her stomach roll again. "I need to tell you some things, but I have to get my head straight first. I'll come if you still want me to stay with you after that." She could bury herself in work. She'd done that for years. Work was an addiction, too. At least it was for her.

"Okay. Let me work on getting you a place to get your head straight. I'll call you back."

Honor disconnected the phone and stood up.

She walked out of the kitchen and was slammed backward. Her arms flew out to her side, and she grabbed at the air, trying to stop the fall to the floor. She landed on her elbows, her head jerked backward, and bounced on the patterned linoleum. Stars shimmered as the edges of her sight went black.

6

Sage put his shoulder holster on now that he wasn't mopping. The flop of the forty-five against his arm had been annoying when he was bent over and scrubbing the floor with the sorry mop he'd found in the kitchen. He listened to Honor speak quietly in the other room. She'd really lost it there for a bit. He had no idea what to do or say. The worry and frustration had manifested in him having problems talking, so after the first attempt, he'd just kept his mouth shut and held her. God, he felt useless. He felt the tears soak into his shirt as he held her tight and rubbed her back in a vain attempt to soothe away some of the pain that had to have caused the breakdown. He wanted to help, to be able to do something more than a hug, but that wasn't his skill set. So, he just held on to her while she released the tears.

By the time she'd pulled herself together, he'd gone through the mental exercises Jeremiah and his speech therapists had taught him. If he could have slayed whatever demons were chasing the poor woman, he would have. Her gut-wrenching cries stabbed at him. He had no defenses against her tears and wanted nothing more than to chase away what was causing her pain.

Sage spun at the sound of the apartment door crashing open. The first man through the door rushed straight forward, and Sage was ready for everything except the knife. He bent backward as the knife flicked forward. The man powered ahead with an attack putting Sage on the defensive. Another man behind him entered the front room and yelled, "The woman is in the kitchen."

Sage used the distraction to get his feet under him and crouched. When knife-dude came at him again, he was ready. He sidestepped the thrust and caught the man's wrist, pushing him forward, using the man's momentum against him. As he passed Sage, Sage used his grip on the man's wrist to snap his arm backward. Keeping the elbow straight, he heard the shoulder, or maybe it was the elbow, dislocate as the man fell to his knees. Joints were the weakest points, and Sage loved using them to his advantage.

He spun and drew his weapon. The other man was overweight by about a hundred pounds, but those types of brutes were hard to bring down. Fat protected the body even if it slowed the fucker down. The man stopped, hands in the air. "Who the f-fuck sent you?" *Son of a bitch!*

The asshole sneered at him. "We want the woman." Sage slammed the man in the side of the head with the butt end of his weapon, sending him to the floor. He patted down fat-boy and then pushed knife-dude to the floor from his knees before he patted him down, too. No weapons and no wallets, so no identification. Glancing again at the knife-wielding fucker to make sure he was down and staying down, Sage grabbed his coat on the way to the kitchen. Honor was pulling herself up when he reached her. He grabbed her and his phone, and they scrambled out of the apartment and into his truck. He was driving away less than ten seconds later.

"Who were they?" Sage raged as he turned at the block's end.

"What? I don't know!" Honor tucked into the corner of the seat, pushing against the door.

Fuck. Fuck, fuck. Sage pulled his foot off the accelerator and reduced his speed to go with the flow of traffic. He grabbed his phone from the seat and pressed redial.

"Hey, you have to give me a couple minutes." Jewell laughed.

"We were attacked in her apartment."

"On it." Zane's voice was on the line.

"Subjects have a dislocated shoulder and a head injury." He described the damage he'd done to the bastards.

"Notifying DPD. Where are you?"

Sage snapped, "On the road."

"Did you get any information from them?" Zane punched the question right back at him.

"No. No identification. One baited me, telling me they were there for the woman. Honor doesn't know them." He glanced over at her. She had her arms wrapped around herself and looked as pale as a person could get without turning into a ghost. Her eyes were wide, and she stared at him as he continued, "It could have been related to the earlier incident. A man at the bar said the punks I took care of had friends."

Zane made a noise of agreement, and Sage could hear typing in the background. "I have a visual on their car," Jewell said.

"How do you know it's their car?"

"The only thing to park down the street from the bar in the last five minutes. I have the bar's video feed from the earlier incident. Playing it at ten times ... There. There they are."

"Facial rec?" Honor said from where she'd tucked herself.

"It's dark, but I'm trying."

Honor looked at the phone, "Edit the—"

Jewell laughed. "I'm on it. God, I missed you."

Zane gruffed, "We need to find a place for you two to hole up."

Honor closed her eyes and leaned her head against the window. Sage turned and headed east. "I'm taking her someplace safe." He knew every person in Bienvenu, and they could be there by morning.

SAGE SLOWED the truck and pulled in front of the small restaurant in Venice, Louisiana. "Be right back."

Honor nodded and closed her eyes. She hadn't spoken except to tell him to pull over. Twice. The woman had to be heaving up her stomach lining by then. She was shivering and wore his jacket. He'd driven without air conditioning, trying to keep her warm. He'd lived with a drunk, and he knew it would get worse before it got better. Either that or Honor would start drinking again. That would be her call. Not his. He'd learned that, too.

"Morning, can I help you, love?" The waitress stood up from the stool she'd been sitting on.

"Morning. May I get an order to go?" Sage looked up at the menu above the passthrough kitchen window. "Biscuits, scrambled eggs. Milk, a bottle of water, and a coffee." He glanced back at the truck. Honor hadn't moved.

"Want gravy, jelly, or sausage on those biscuits?" the woman asked.

"No, ma'am. Plain." He didn't know what Honor could stomach, so he kept it generic.

"That'll be seven-twenty-eight."

Sage pulled out his wallet and handed the woman a ten. "Keep the change."

"Well, thank you." The woman put the money he owed into the till, pocketed the rest before she smiled, and headed into the kitchen.

Not more than five minutes later, Sage was back in the truck. He opened the biscuits. "You need to eat something. This is just bread. There are some scrambled eggs. This is milk." He sat the containers between them.

Honor swallowed hard and closed her eyes. "I can't."

"I know you think that, but your stomach will shred if you don't have something. A little bread. Please." She looked like death warmed over. The dark circles under her eyes were vivid against her pale skin. He lifted the box and offered it to her.

She sat up and groaned. "My head is killing me."

"I know." She probably had a concussion from the bar and what happened at her apartment. "Just a bite or two. We're almost there."

"Your house," she said, acknowledging for the first time that she'd heard what he'd told her as they were leaving Dallas. She pushed her brown hair from her face.

"Yes." He was really worried about her physical

condition. She was shaking, which could be from withdrawal or lack of food.

"I don't know who they were," she said. Her hand shook wildly as she broke off a small piece of the biscuit. She divided that piece further and placed a tiny bit on her tongue.

"I didn't mean to yell at you." He felt like shit about that.

"Doesn't matter." She shrugged.

Yeah, it really did. With the comments she'd made about hating herself earlier, his being a dick didn't help. He was there to protect her. To get her the help she needed. He needed to call Jeremiah and talk to him. He was way out of his comfort zone. He'd never been assigned a mission like that before. It wasn't the search-and-destroy tactics that he and Smoke had perfected. No, his mission was personal, and in reality, Honor's future depended on him. The pressure he felt was magnified by the fact that there was something ... wounded—no, vulnerable—about her that drew him toward her.

"Water?" He handed her the bottle, but she shook her head.

Sage waited until she'd consumed the small corner she'd torn off before starting the truck and heading south, past Orchard and on to the town where he'd grown up. The old, faded "Welcome to Bienvenu" sign outside the township limits no longer mocked him. It was a damn good feeling. He drove through the town, turned toward the water, and headed to his house. As he pulled up, he smiled a bit. The old gray paint was gone. The new white paint with black hurricane shutters looked damn good and would have made his mom happy. He put the truck into park and got out, going to the passenger side to help Honor down. He found the key to the house where Beau had said he'd put it and helped Honor climb the stairs. The house was elevated twenty-eight feet above sea level, so climbing all those stairs was slow going. The woman was hurting, but she wasn't complaining or mean as Gus had been. But then again, Gus was just a mean person. Period.

He unlocked the door and entered his code into the alarm panel. The house smelled of fresh paint and new wood. Sage glanced around in wonder. The pictures and videos didn't do the home justice. The front-facing windows had a one-hundred-eighty-degree view of the water. A large tanker was making its way north to the ports on the river. It was home.

Honor shivered beside him. "Come on." He

took her to the small bedroom across from what used to be his mom and Gus's room. It had been repainted, and a new queen-sized bedroom suite was all made up and ready. "Bathroom is through there. I don't know if there's any soap or shampoo. I'll get that today."

"I just want to sleep," Honor whispered.

"Okay. I'll let you do that." Walking into the bedroom, he opened the window and pulled the plantation shutter closed, darkening the room. Then he shut the window and locked it. "If you need anything, I'm just a shout away."

"Thanks." Honor moved toward the bed, which Sage took as his cue to leave. He shut the door behind him. Sighing, he turned and gazed at the house. The new tile flooring replaced the ratty old carpeting that had been threadbare in areas. He'd had all new windows installed. Hurricane-force wind resistant. He opened the door to the bedroom, where he sat with his mom as she passed. It had changed the most. Hardwood floors in a light gray color mimicked the wall color. He extended the bedroom taking out two of the smallest rooms and a closet to add a large bathroom and walk-in closet. The bed was a king-sized sleigh bed that wouldn't have fit in the space his mom's full-size bed had been. He'd used his money and connections to get her the best medical care possible, but the cancer had gone too far, and she was too tired to fight in the end. The smell of the medication and death were long gone from the house. But he'd never forget them. Even with the changes he'd made, the memories would still be here. And that ... well, that was okay. Living with your memories, even those that caused pain, and accepting what life had dealt were lessons he'd learned from Jeremiah.

Sage left the bedroom and went out to the front room. The walls between the kitchen, dining room, and living room had been removed, opening the area into one space. White paint on the walls and black furniture on white tiles gave the rooms a masculine feel. Sage couldn't help thinking his mom would have been happy to see the home she'd paid for turned into such a nice house. He walked through the living room and opened the office door. Built-in shelves could hold a library's worth of books. He smiled. His mom also would have loved that. She made the trek to the county library every week with her boys. She loved to read, and they'd all escaped through the stories she'd read to them when they were young.

Sage had sent her books from around the world when he was in the military and after joining Guardian. Those were now arranged on the shelves behind an ultra-modern glass and chrome desk. He left the door open and went back through the living room and outside to the wraparound porch, where two black lacquered rockers were placed under a row of ceiling fans. Sage hit the switch to turn the fans on and sat down on one of the chairs.

He surveyed the property. His mother had worked as a cleaning lady, taking in laundry and sewing to pay for the house. He never knew. He thought the reason she'd stayed was because of Gus. He thought the house was Gus's. It wasn't. The house, that view, was her gift to her boys. Her legacy. His brothers had been okay with him buying them out. They wouldn't come back. But he had. There was still some unfinished business in his past, but he'd made peace with that.

As he watched a freighter head up the river, he heard a vehicle driving down the gravel road. Sage stood and went to the far railing of the porch. A Plaquemines Parish Sheriff's vehicle pulled up beside his truck. Beau got out and waved, ducking back inside the small SUV for a bag and tray of what Sage hoped was coffee.

Beau spoke as he climbed the long flight of stairs to the house. "The notification that the alarm was deactivated hit just as I was picking up my breakfast after working out. What are you doing back down here?"

"I had a job in Dallas, and there was a little detour." Sage shook Beau's free hand. "Please tell me that's coffee. I didn't have time to go to the grocery store in Venice."

Beau blinked at him. "Hot damn! I'm still thrilled you're not stuttering! Brother, that's something. I could tell you were improving when we talked on the phone. So fucking happy for you, man."

Sage smiled. "I still have my moments. Mainly when I'm upset or frustrated."

"Damn, it's good to hear and see you. I brought breakfast burritos and doughnuts. Don't tell Evangeline." Beau sat down in one of the rockers, and Sage took the other. "How did they fix it?"

Sage took a sip of the coffee that Beau handed him. "Man, I had a medical team of specialists. Speech pathologists and I worked with different machines. I could talk without stuttering when someone else was speaking. So, this device would echo my words back into my ear. It was freaky and, damn, so freeing. That started it, but it took work and a fuck-ton of therapy. Gus and growing up here figured into it more than I thought."

A slow wide smile spread across Beau's face. "Never knew anyone who went to therapy. You going to start sharing your emotions with me, now?"

"Fuck no." Sage laughed and took the burrito Beau offered him. "The house is better than I thought it could be."

"Ahead of schedule, too. I don't know where you got those guys or how much you paid them to camp out here until the house was done, but dude, they are so much better than any contractor you could get here."

"Let me know if you need them."

"I will, especially if this storm hits." Beau unwrapped his burrito and took a bite.

"Storm?" Sage paused with his food unwrapped and halfway to his mouth.

Beau nodded as he finished chewing his food. "Right now, she's a Tropical Storm with signs of intensifying. The spaghetti models are all over the place, but we're in the cone of probability. Hopefully, it keeps moving east. I don't want to wish a storm on anyone, but ..."

Sage nodded and took a bite of his food. Nobody wished a storm on anyone, but no one wanted to be hit by one, either. Thankfully, his construction crew had reinforced the pilings of the house and made structural changes to fortify it against hurricane-force winds.

"How long you staying?" Beau asked, taking a break from his food.

"I don't know. I'm doing an escort-protection gig right now." He wasn't going to go into the details. Beau would understand.

"Now?" Beau looked over his shoulder to the wide-open front door.

Sage nodded his head. "Needed a quiet out-of-the-way place to lay low."

"Anything I need to know about?" Beau's stare turned deadly serious.

"No." Sage chuckled. "No worries for anyone but her and me."

Beau's eyebrows lifted. "Her? Oh ..." The way he said the question made Sage laugh. Just like Beau to pull an elementary school response out of his hat.

"Man, what are you, ten?"

"According to Evangeline, I'm permanently stuck with a twelve-year-old's mentality. I disagree."

"No?" Sage crumpled up the tinfoil that had wrapped the burrito.

"Nope. I'm at least fourteen because ... sex, you know?"

Sage damn near spit out his coffee. "Jesus, Beau." Sage wiped his mouth as Beau's laughter surrounded them.

"Evangeline is heading north today. She's taking the kids to the zoo and the aquarium. She can pick you up some basics." Beau leaned back and took a bite of the jelly-filled doughnut he pulled from the bag. Pointing at the bag, telling Sage to take one without saying a word.

"That would be nice." Sage pulled out his wallet and took out five one-hundred-dollar bills. "For her, gas and admission into the zoo, aquarium, and whatever."

Beau took a sip of his coffee. "You rich?"

Sage dropped the money on Beau's leg. "I haven't had anything to spend my money on, so I have a good amount saved." Guardian had paid him through his and his mom's treatments and footed all the medical expenses for both.

"Does Guardian have any openings?"

Sage chuckled. "I'm sure they do. Not sure you'd be able to stay here, though."

Beau sighed. "Couldn't leave Mom and Dad or Evangeline's family."

"You're lucky." Sage wished he had a family connection. He and his half-brothers talked, but they weren't close. Hell, he was closer to Beau than he was to his brothers.

"Well, you're family, too. Who'd ever think my mom and dad would adopt a straggly lil white boy like you."

"Straggly? Like you weren't as skinny as a bean pole."

Beau laughed. "Man, I could eat all day and not gain an ounce." He slapped his flat stomach. "Those were the days."

Sage snorted. "If you're fishing for compliments, go talk to your wife."

"Probably should. She's going to want the gossip before she heads north. I'll let Mom and Dad know you're in town. They'll expect you for dinner tonight. It's Sunday."

Sage glanced at the open doorway. "Probably not going to happen. Not sure what the schedule is here. Will you pass on my apologies?" He had no idea what was coming down the pipe with Honor's alcohol issue, and Guardian could have him on the road at any time.

"I will. Not sure it'll work, but I will." Beau stood up and stretched. "You'll let me know if this protection gig becomes my issue, right?"

"You know it." Sage stood and extended his hand.

Beau pulled him in and slapped his back. "Happy for you, brother."

"Thanks. Give Evangeline and the kids a hug for me."

"Hug them yourself when they show up this afternoon." Beau laughed and made his way down the stairs. "Any special requests?"

"None that I can ... Hey, Beau?"

Beau turned and looked up at him from the bottom of the stairs. "What you need, man? Name it."

"Clothes. Women's clothes. She's a bit shorter than Evangeline and doesn't have the curves your wife has, but she's about the same size. Basic stuff. We left in a hurry."

Beau rubbed the back of his neck. "But it's not my problem."

Sage laughed. "Not your problem."

Beau lifted a hand. "Evie might skip the zoo to get here sooner. You know she's going to want to know everything."

"I'll tell her what I can." Which wasn't much.

"Ha! She'll have all the deets in less than a half hour."

"She wishes!" Sage laughed and waved as Beau got into his patrol car.

7

Jewell stared at the computer screen and then moved her gaze to the enhanced photo she'd run through the facial recognition database. "I had to have modified the faces in some way."

"What?" Zane asked from behind her.

"I used a graphic program to lighten the faces so the facial recognition program would have more to work with. AI fills in the blanks with the most likely feature."

"Okay. Why do you think you've modified the faces?"

"Look." Jewell pointed to the picture facial rec had popped on. "A ninety percent match."

"That's good, right?" Zane asked as he sat down beside her.

"No. That's *not* good. If this is right, those guys weren't local bikers. They're known associates of the Russian Mafia." She turned toward Zane and watched his reaction.

His eyes narrowed, and he stared at the screen. "If you follow that line of thought, how would they know where Honor was?"

"Wait." Jewell dropped her feet to the floor and turned her chair toward her husband. "Don't I want to know why?"

Zane turned to look at her. "Honor can tell us why. We need to know how."

Jewell pulled a pencil out of the drawer. It was too early to have any stuck in her messy bun. She put the eraser in her mouth for a second before she jumped. "Honor, when she was drunk, she said she should have died in the attack." The pencil slipped from Jewell's hand and clattered to the floor. "You don't think she was in bed with the Russian Mafia? That Richard used them when he orchestrated the Siege?"

"That is a supposition without facts." Zane shook his head. "Until we have facts, we work on the how. When we know that, we can talk to Honor and ask the questions to which we already know the answers."

"To make sure she's on the level with us."

Zane nodded. "I know she's a friend, babe, but if she's involved with the Bratva, we need answers."

"I need her computers turned on."

"We know a guy who can do that," Zane said as he punched a number into the computer.

"Yo, what's up," Sage answered the phone on the first ring.

"Sage, is Honor near you?"

"Sleeping down the hall. What do you need?"

Zane explained the tenuous link between the men who attacked them at Honor's apartment to the Bratva as Jewell chewed on a new pencil. *This can't be right*. Honor was her go-to on the night shift. The woman was dedicated and worked damn hard at keeping their systems safe. Jewell tuned back into Zane's conversation.

"Let me know when you're back inside with the computers." Zane put the phone on mute. "What are you going to look for?"

Jewell shook her head. "This feels like an invasion of her privacy."

"She signed an agreement when she signed on with us. Anything on those computers can be searched because she's worked for Guardian. Even ten years from now, we have the legal authority to make sure none of our information is out there."

Jewell nodded. "I know." Still. "She wouldn't be careless. She'd delete any information she didn't want anyone to see, then try to obscure any memory that could still retain any data. Anything I need won't be on the laptops. I need inside her primary computer."

"Can you do that without having her password?" Zane glanced at her.

"She's freaking brilliant. It won't be easy, but yeah. I think I can. It'll take time. We're talking days, if not weeks." Jewell pushed her bangs out of her face. "We probably need to brief this up the chain of command."

Zane smiled. "We do. In the meantime, she can stay with Sage in the middle of nowhere, and we'll ask questions when we know there's any reason for concern. As it is, she's drying out and getting healthy. We'll bring her in for questioning if we need to do so. If not, we can hope she's agreeable to counseling so we can clear her to come back to work."

"I'm back with the box." Sage's voice caused

Jewel to jump. She'd forgotten he'd gone for the computer.

Zane unmuted the line. "That's your cue, babe."

Jewell nodded. "Okay, first we'll need to power it up …"

HONOR GASPED AND WOKE UP. Where … She jerked as she looked around the unfamiliar room—Sage's *house*. Honor shivered and swallowed hard. She was soaked with sweat, but the nightmare that still danced on her terrified nerve endings kept her under the covers. God, the muddled mess of the dream mixed the biker that had grabbed her with memories of Dean and a computer monster trying to devour her.

Honor drew several breaths before she sat up. The ever-present headache throbbed undeterred as she glanced at the bedside clock. Six thirty. God, she'd slept all day and was still so tired.

Honor made her way into the bathroom and washed up as best as possible. Though the shower looked appealing, she didn't see soap or shampoo. She put her jeans and shirt back on afterward but didn't bother with her socks or shoes. As she slowly opened the door, a heavenly smell reached her, and she followed the aroma to the kitchen, where Sage sat at a small table.

"Hey, would you like some soup?" He stood and headed toward the range.

"Thank you." She glanced around the kitchen. "Water?"

"Bottled in the fridge," Sage said as he ladled her a bowl of soup.

She opened the fridge and grabbed a water, taking it back to the table and sitting across from where his dinner awaited him.

"This is homemade cream of chicken soup. The bread is homemade, too. A friend of mine told his parents I was back, and they stopped by with this."

Honor drew in a lungful of the delicious aroma. "It smells really good."

"It is. Miss Anita makes the best food." Sage sat down across from her. "How are you feeling?"

Honor chuffed. "Like I've been hit by a truck." She wasn't joking. "Do you have anything for a headache?"

Sage nodded. "I do. You probably want some-thing in your stomach before you take it, though."

Honor picked up the spoon and dipped it into the thick golden soup. She tasted it and closed her eyes. She hadn't had anything but fast food since ... She opened her eyes and put the spoon down.

"What just happened?" Sage asked as he buttered a thick slice of bread.

Honor jumped. "What?"

"You were eating, and then you thought of something, and you stopped." He didn't look at her. Instead, he continued to eat.

Honor leaned back in her chair and ran her finger along a carved groove in the tabletop. "Have you ever done something you'll regret until the day you die?"

Sage lifted his eyes to hers. "I've done a lot I'm not proud of. But that's a lot of regret."

Honor glanced down at her broken nails as they followed the etching. "Yeah."

"That's why you drink? This regret?"

Honor flicked her eyes to him, but he wasn't looking at her. He was eating. "A simplistic view, but ... yeah."

"Eat some more," Sage said, pushing a slice of bread her way. Honor took the bread and tore a small piece off it. She dipped it in the soup and let it dissolve in her mouth. It was warm, and the flavor was heavenly. She swallowed that piece and tore another small hunk of bread from the slice. As she dipped it into the soup, she asked, "Has Jewell called?"

Sage nodded. "She did. Some heavy stuff is happening, and she's been called away to help work it. With such a limited full-time CCS staff, she couldn't say no. I'm afraid we're adrift here until she's freed up, and then we'll know which way to go."

Honor nodded and ate the bread. "I'm sorry for being an inconvenience." She glanced at Sage.

He looked up at her from his food. "Honor, I don't know what's going on with you, but you're not an inconvenience. Tomorrow, I'm going to introduce you to a man who helped me. You can talk to him or not. Your choice. He's Guardian and a shrink, but I trust him with my life. Having someone to talk to, to make sense of the crap jumbled up in your head, might be a good thing. It helped me."

Honor stopped eating and stared at Sage. She didn't want to meet anyone, especially now. She sighed, "He's here?"

Sage chuckled. "No, we'll do a video chat if

you're up to it or a phone call. If we need to wait another day or two, that's all right, too."

Honor nodded and picked apart the bread, dipping each small piece into the soup before she ate it. She stopped and looked at Sage, who was scrolling on his phone. She had so many questions, but the unrelenting urge to run away, to find a bottle and crawl in it, stomped on top of those questions and muddled them in her head. Finally, she blurted out one before it was mashed back into the brain fog enveloping her. "He helped you?"

Sage blinked and looked up. He smiled, and her eyes caught on that brilliant flash. "He did. I used to stutter." Perhaps in another time, with different circumstances, she could have reveled in admiring how attractive he was without the quagmire of questions demanding the attention of her rambling mind. Honor wrapped her arms around herself because she was cold. What had he said? Stuttering.

"Why? I mean, was it a childhood thing? The stuttering?"

"In medical terms, I had a psychogenic speech disorder. My stuttering was caused by a psychological process. I was lucky it wasn't caused by the TBI I received while serving in the military. It started when I was recovering from that incident, so the military assumed the explosion caused it and was permanent. Most people wrote me off after I was medically discharged, but a few didn't. Guardian didn't."

Honor took in the information. The man in front of her looked completely relaxed and in charge of his life. She couldn't imagine him as anything else. As he glanced down at his phone, his long dark lashes almost brushed his cheek. He was handsome. That much wiggled its way through her misery. However, there was more to him than his looks. She could tell from how he talked and moved that he possessed a strength beyond physical brawn. It seemed like everything he did came effortlessly—from the simple yet confident set of his jawline to how casually he sat scrolling through his phone. His demeanor carried an air of authority. She'd seen men like him before in Guardian's hallways. He knew what needed to be done and had all tools for completing tasks. Honor closed her eyes. Yeah, he was attractive, but she shoved that thought down and closed her eyes. She had other priorities. Things that brought her thoughts of him to a screaming halt.

She sighed and rubbed her arms again. Her head ached.

Sage stood up. "I'll get you some pain relievers."

Honor chuffed. "A bottle of vodka would help."

Sage stopped and turned around. "I don't have any alcohol in the house. I don't allow it on the premises. My mother lived with a man who was an alcoholic. He was mean—vicious mean. The bar is five miles down the road if you want a drink. You can't miss it. I'm not going to stop you." He headed to the cabinet and pulled down a bottle of pain relievers. He shook two out into his hand as she watched.

Honor blinked, and her jaw dropped open. "You're not going to try to stop me?"

Sage shook his head and returned with the pain relievers. "No one can make you stop drinking. It has to be something you want. Ask yourself what made you pour that vodka out last night."

Honor glanced down at the ring on her finger. She extended her fingers and looked at the broken nails. In her mind's eye, she saw her reflection in the mirror at the bar. "A lot of things."

"Use them to make yourself stronger than the

desire for a drink." He put the tablets on the table and took his bowl to the sink.

Honor took the pain relievers and stood up. She walked her bowl and the plate with half a slice of bread still on it to the sink. "My friend brought over some things you might be able to use. I had her buy you some clothes, too. I have no idea if the sizes are right, but the bags are over there."

Honor stared at the bag. "She knows about me?"

"No. She knows I'm helping someone and that you needed a few things. She tried to get more out of me." Sage laughed. "Evangeline is a tiger."

When Honor glanced up at him, she could see the emotion in his eyes. He cared for the woman. She was probably as pretty as he was handsome. Looking away, Honor moved over to the bags while wondering what it would feel like to have a man really care for her. She picked up the bags and focused back on him. "Thank you."

"Not a problem. I'll be up for a while if you want to visit. If not, have a good evening, and I'll see you in the morning."

Honor nodded and headed down the hallway. The bags were heavy, and by the time she reached the door to her room, she was exhausted. She slid the bags inside the room, shut the door, and stripped as she walked over to the bed. Then she slipped under the covers and closed her eyes. Maybe she'd wake up, and the nightmare her life had become would disappear.

8

Sage woke with the sun. He'd eaten and checked in with Zane before he heard Honor stirring, and when she came out of the bedroom, he was not expecting what he saw. Wearing a yellow sundress and a white sweater, she'd brushed and braided her hair. The thick braid rested over her shoulder, and the end of it almost touched her elbow. She looked pale but so much better than yesterday and the day before. It made sense that he felt drawn to take care of her. His protective instinct had kicked into overdrive around her because she was vulnerable. Right now, Honor needed somebody to look after her— someone who could keep the world at bay and give her a chance to heal.

"Good morning. Would you like something to eat?" Sage motioned to the kitchen.

Honor lifted her eyes to him, and they were terrified. "I can't stop." She extended her hand. The tremors moved her hand and arm violently. "I'm scared."

Sage was beside her in a heartbeat and put his arm around her waist. "When did it start."

"After I braided my hair." Her entire body was shaking as he helped her to the sofa. "Here. Just sit down. I'm calling for help."

"I don't want to leave. I don't want to go anywhere." Honor curled in on herself.

He dialed Jeremiah's number and prayed the man wasn't in with a patient yet.

"Dr. Wheeler."

"I need some help."

"Are you okay?"

"Not me. Alcohol-dependent person. Whole body tremors."

"How much have they consumed."

"Nothing for almost three days."

"Ah. Withdrawal. Vomiting? Nausea? Hallucinations?" Jeremiah asked.

"Honor, any vomiting, nausea, or hallucinations?"

"Nausea," Honor said, her teeth clattering.

"I heard. Listen, if she was my patient, I could prescribe something to help ease the withdrawal, but not without examining her. As it is, these symptoms could last up to seventy-two hours."

"What can I do, doc?"

"Keep her comfortable. There's something you need to watch out for. If she exhibits any signs of delirium, like a lack of awareness of her current reality, if she starts hallucinating, you get her to a doctor fast. It only happens in one percent of the cases of alcohol withdrawal, but you need to know."

Sage ran his hand through his hair. Shit, hadn't she been through enough already? He hated this for her. "Okay."

"Call me when you can talk. I'll answer if I can."

"Will do." He hung up the phone and grabbed a fake fur blanket from the back of the couch. He put it over Honor, and she burrowed into it.

"I'm sorry," she murmured through her shivers.

Sage got a pillow for her from the loveseat. "Don't be. The doc said this was part of the process of drying out."

"Fuck." Honor spat the word out. "I picked a great day to stop drinking."

Sage chuckled. "That's a line from an old movie."

Honor groaned. "Airplane."

Sage sat down beside her. "Old movie buff?"

She nodded, although he only saw the top of her head move. The rest of her was curled under the blanket. "Cold."

"I'll get you more covers." Sage was back in less than thirty seconds with two big quilts. He put them over her and pulled down the fur far enough to see her. She opened her eyes and stared up at him. "I'm going to sit right over there. If you need me, just say my name."

She nodded and pushed deeper under the blanket. Sage moved across the room and sat down. Fuck, she was going through hell. He leaned back and stared at the small huddle.

He'd laid awake last night thinking about their conversations while they were in the apartment. Could she be involved with the Bratva as Jewell and Zane suspected?

People who hate themselves don't like to look in mirrors. That was what she'd said. Why would she hate herself? What would cause a woman to crawl into a bottle and stay there? What would cause her to crawl back out? Who was the enemy she was facing? Sage ground his teeth together. He'd like to find whomever or whatever that fucker was and pound it into the ground.

He turned his head to look out the expansive windows. She was a tiny thing, and yeah, he knew women could be ruthless and cold-blooded, but he didn't get that vibe from Honor. What he got from her was a lot of fear, regret, and sadness. He wondered what she looked like when she smiled. He bet her eyes lit up and her face flushed. Her brown hair and blue eyes were a unique combination. There was something about her that reached out and got his attention. Or maybe he was just a damn fool. He sighed and got comfortable. It would be a long day. Longer for her.

HONOR WOKE AGAIN, awash in sweat. She pushed off the heavy blankets and sat up, swiping the hair out of her face and swatting the messy braid to her back. God, she ached.

"Water?"

She jerked around at Sage's voice. "How long did I sleep?"

"About six hours. And I'd call it thrashing more than sleeping." After he handed her a water bottle, she leaned back against the cushion. "Are you feeling better?" Sage moved to the seat across from her and sat down.

"I fill like shit, I ache all over, and I'm exhausted ... so, yeah. A lot better."

Sage fought a smile, and Honor gave herself props for being able to joke when she felt like death warmed over. She tried to take the top off the bottle but didn't have the strength. "Here." Sage was across the room and had the bottle opened before she could think to ask for help.

"Thank you." She took a sip of the water, and her stomach didn't revolt, so she took another. God, she was exhausted. "I felt better this morning. I took a shower, braided my hair, and then, bam, I couldn't stop shaking. I feel like a vise has squished me."

Sage nodded. "Do you want something to eat?"

She sighed. "I don't, and I'm too tired."

"Easy to fix. I'll put soup in a mug and bring it out here. You can rest"

Honor smiled at him and watched as he

headed into the kitchen. He was determined to get her to eat. She stared at him as he moved around the kitchen and sighed. He was a beautiful man with a graceful way about him. Like he knew where everything was all the time. His body was like a movie star's. Wide shoulders, narrow waist. She sighed and closed her eyes. Just like a movie star, the man who had rescued her and was helping her fight her demons was too good to be true. She knew why Sage was taking care of her. As a favor to a friend. God, Jewell.

Honor swallowed hard and thought of her friend. How could she tell Jewell what had happened all those years ago and what had happened that day? She knew why the building was blown up. It was all because of her.

"Honor?"

She jumped and almost knocked the mug of soup from Sage's hand. "Sorry." Slowly, she pulled herself back up and adjusted the blankets. Sage handed her the cup, and she sipped it. "This is so good."

"I agree," Sage said, sitting in his chair with his mug.

"I hope Jewell is paying you enough to watch over me." She stared at her mug.

"Why do you say that?" Sage asked from across the room.

Honor shrugged. "I think I'm a lot of work right now."

Sage chuckled. "You're more worry than work."

She glanced over in his direction. "Worry?"

He took a sip of his soup before he answered. "Gus, the man my mother lived with, never had tremors. I was expecting the usual, and you go and freak me out with tremors."

Honor dropped her eyes and stared at the white ceramic mug in her hand. "I never want to feel that way again."

"Then don't. You're in charge of how you feel."

Honor rolled her head and looked at him. "Not right now, I'm not."

Sage snorted. "True, the alcohol leaving your system is in charge, but once it's gone, it's all on you."

Honor stared at him for a moment as his words settled around her. It was all on her. It was time she faced that fact. "I'm the reason they blew up the headquarters building that day."

Sage's head snapped up. "I'm sorry, what?"

Honor held the cup and sniffed back a tear. "It's a long story, but he told me if I didn't help them, they'd make me and everyone else at Guardian pay."

"Richard Berkley?" Sage cocked his head as if the words she was saying were in a foreign language or muddled.

"No. Dean Benedict. Who's Richard Berkley?"

"Who's Dean Benedict?" Sage asked in return, then held up a hand. "Wait, we need to start from the beginning. Who's Dean Benedict, and what does he have to do with the Siege?"

Honor blinked at him. "The Siege? Is that what everyone is calling it?"

Sage nodded. "They took out Guardian Headquarters, laid siege to the Annex, and shot down a plane."

Honor stared at him. "You're not making sense. How could he have orchestrated that in less than twenty-four hours?"

"Who?"

"Dean Benedict. Aren't you listening to me?" Honor put the soup mug on the floor and twisted to look at Sage. "Dean Benedict used me to build him a program. He stole it from me, and horrible things happened. I covered it up because I loved the people at Guardian, and I didn't want them to know I screwed up. I worked my ass off, making amends for that night even though they didn't know I was the cause of the breach in security. Well, not me, but the program Dean stole."

Sage stood up. "Okay, you got a lot of things wrong. First, Richard Berkley orchestrated that tactical nightmare and had plenty of help, but not from the Bratva."

"The Bratva? You mean the Russian hacker who used my program years ago?" Honor stared up at him. "You aren't making any sense."

Sage stopped and looked at her. "Honor, do you know where you're at?"

"What? I'm on your couch. Beyond that, no, because I was too damn sick to care to watch where you drove."

"Right." Sage nodded. "We need to go."

"Go where?" Honor squeaked when he whipped back the blankets.

"To the ER. Jeremiah said to watch for breaks from reality."

He scooped her up in his arms, and she scrambled to grab his neck to stay upright. "Sage, put me down. I know what I'm doing and what I'm saying."

He turned his head to look directly at her. "Do you?" His eyes searched hers.

She stared right back at him. "I do. I feel like crap, but I'm not having a break from reality."

"But you're not making any sense either." Sage walked her back to the couch and put her down.

Honor deflated. Any energy she had from the nap was long gone. But she needed to do it. To get it over with so she could face the consequences of her decisions. "Look, get Jewell on the line. I'm too tired to deny my part in this any longer. I'll tell you everything, but I'm only doing it once."

She watched as Sage pulled out his cell and dialed. Zane answered. Honor adored Zane. He took such good care of Jewell. You could tell the man loved her with every fiber of his soul.

She waited until Jewell came online. "What's up?"

"I need to make some confessions to you. Sage obviously doesn't understand what I'm saying."

There was silence on the other end of the line before Zane spoke. "Honor, to protect you and us, I'm going to have Sage read you your Miranda rights."

"Is this being recorded?" She knew that the conversation was, but she wanted to hear it out loud.

"Yes," Jewell replied.

"I know my Constitutional rights against self-incrimination, and I waive all rights at this time." Honor closed her eyes. "Sage, please come over here. I'm too tired to yell toward the phone."

Sage shifted his position from the chair to the couch. He sat the phone between them. Honor began. "Before I started work with Guardian, I was working as a data entry specialist. I needed to pay rent, so I took whatever job I could. I met a man. Dean Benedict. We started talking, dating, and he spent time at my apartment." Honor looked up and frowned. "I never went to his. Funny what you remember looking back."

Sage put his hand on hers. "About Benedict."

The warmth of his hand on hers was fleeting but enough to push her back into the right train of thought. "Right. During that time, I started working for Guardian. He poked fun at my programming skills. He bet me I couldn't make a program that burrowed through firewalls without being detected. I bet him I could. I worked on that program for over a year. He stole it from me one night when I was working late. I came home in time to catch him. He admitted he only had sex with me because he wanted the program." Tears streamed down her eyes. "I told him how dangerous the program could be in the wrong hands. I begged him not to take it. He hit me."

"You said you ran into the door jamb. You had a bruise that covered half your face." Jewell supplied.

"Yeah." Honor acknowledged. "I tried to cover the bruise up, and I built a program to defeat the Nutcracker. I waited, watched, and listened, but I never saw it, never read reports about it until one night when I was working late. Archangel was flying with your brother Jason, Archangel's wife's car was attacked, and Jason's fiancée's trailer was blown-up."

"What?" Jewell gasped.

"I saw it that night. The Nutcracker. It was already inside our system. They'd gotten in and had found the information they'd used that night. I watched as the Nutcracker moved toward other information. I killed it. I spiked the computer that was controlling it and covered it up. I was so afraid I'd lose my job. That I'd lose everything."

"You stopped them from getting more information," Jewell said.

"But it was my program that gave them what they had!" Honor dropped her head back on the couch and swiped at the tears. "I'm the reason all that happened."

"And you're the reason it didn't get any worse. If you didn't act fast, Guardian could have been decimated," Jewell argued.

She turned toward the beautiful man with caring eyes. "But don't you see, ultimately, I *was* the reason. When Dean found me the day before the headquarters building blew up, he tried to force me to go with him. He said if I didn't build another program for him, he'd make me and everyone at Guardian pay. I was so scared. He wasn't the man I remembered. He had a long, jagged scar across the bridge of his nose, and he'd aged so much. His mistake was that he stopped me outside the coffee shop across the street from headquarters. He bumped into me on the way out of the shop. He grabbed my arm, and God, I swear he was as surprised as I was, at least for a second. I screamed at him to let me go and jammed my heel into his foot. A random guy on the street stopped him from following me. I ran to headquarters and didn't leave. I slept in one of the converted offices. I was too afraid to go home. And then, when the building blew up ... I thought you were dead, too. It collapsed on you. I made my way out, went home, got my computers, clothes, and money, and I left."

"Someone reported you got out alive. That's why I've been looking for you. Those deaths weren't on you, Honor. Richard Berkley was the mastermind of the attack on Guardian. I have indisputable proof." Jewell said quietly. "And that's why the Bratva was at your apartment in Dallas two nights ago."

Honor gasped, "What?"

"Honor, what's the password to your primary computer," Jewell asked.

Honor spouted it off. "Why?"

"Because I have a clone of it in my office. We were afraid you were working with the Bratva. We had to know."

"No. I couldn't do that to us." Honor's gut dropped. "I had no idea Dean would take my program, Jewell."

"I know, sweetie. Look, I'm going to bounce around in your computer and do a forensic exam on all the memory. Anything I need to watch out for?"

"Yeah, I have a mini-Godzilla installed. The password to turn him off is Jewell fucking rocks pound sign and the numerals one nine four seven three two zero dollar sign. No spaces. Capital J only."

"Got it. She's working it. Do you know how they found you?" Zane asked.

"No, but I blacked out and lost two days. Have her check my other computers to see if I went online."

"I don't have those." Jewell popped back into the conversation.

Honor sat up and held her head in her hands. "I could check if you think you can trust me."

Jewell sighed. "I trust you, sweetie, but we have to follow protocol."

"I know. Sage can get them for you. I don't have the strength to climb the stairs." Honor looked at Sage. He nodded and headed out of the house. "I know I fucked up, and I know you'll have to fire me for what I did that night, but God, I'm so fucking relieved. I wasn't the reason headquarters was taken down. And that makes me sound pathetic, doesn't it." She picked up Sage's phone. "I'm so sorry."

"Honor, we don't know what the ramifications are in this situation. Neither do you. Until you hear otherwise, you're a member in good standing with Guardian." Zane's voice was soft but firm. "Our big question now is why the Bratva wants you and what type of program they're trying to create."

Honor looked up as Sage came back inside carrying her two laptops. "Whatever it is, it can't be good."

"You can say that again." Jewell agreed. "I'll put feelers out with my contacts that lurk on the dark web. I'd ask you to do the same, Honor, but ..."

"I know. I'm under lock and key until you can run a forensics check on all my computers. You'll need my passwords for the other computers." Honor listed them off for Jewell.

She watched as Sage started up her computer and knew Jewell was taking over. She closed her eyes. Thank God.

"This one is already on, Jewell."

Honor sat up. "What?"

"Yeah." Sage turned it so he could see the face. "It says you need to plug it in." Sage held up both cords, and Honor pointed to the black one. "That's the cord." She watched as Sage plugged in her oldest computer.

"Turn the other one on, please." Jewell requested as Honor stared at the computer.

Honor sat back down. She'd never leave her computer running. That had to be a result of her blackout. Computer security was her forte. Leaving that machine running was a huge mistake. Well, compared to the other mistakes she'd made, maybe not *that* big.

"Okay, we're in. Standby. We'll be in contact." Zane terminated the conversation, and Honor closed her eyes. She might be out of a job and facing jail time, but the pressure weighing on her, pushing her down, felt lighter. Not gone, but lighter.

9

Sage heard the sound of the door across from him open and jolted awake. The house didn't creak as it once did, but he could hear the soft shuffle of feet heading toward the kitchen ... No, the front door.

Sage slid out of bed and put on his jeans, commando. He zipped up and headed to the front door. Was she trying to leave? How far did she think she'd get? He opened the door and stepped out onto the porch.

"I didn't mean to wake you. I couldn't sleep," Honor said from his right. He glanced over and saw her in one of the rocking chairs. She was wearing a pair of jeans and a t-shirt. No shoes or socks.

Sage scratched his chest and yawned. "I would have been up in a couple of minutes anyway." He padded over and dropped into the rocking chair beside her. "Sunrises are nice, but since we face west, the sunsets are better. How are you feeling?"

Honor made a sound of agreement. "Better at times and worse at times. My body isn't happy with me. I still have a headache. I have the urge to drink. Man, do I, but I think getting everything off my chest yesterday helped. Mentally." She pushed the chair with her toe and set her rocker in motion. "If I haven't said thank you for rescuing me and taking care of me, thank you. I know you're just doing a job, but what you've done, what could have happened if you hadn't been there? Well, nightmares are made of that type of thinking." Honor wrapped her arms around herself and shuddered.

"You're more than a job, Honor." He hated that she thought that of herself. She was his duty, true, but she was quickly becoming more than that. She sparked his interest and his protective energies and had even invaded his thoughts. The feeling of helplessness when she was huddled under the blankets fighting her demons stoked the urge to protect her, but also something a little baser than protection. She stirred him in a way he hadn't thought possible in such a short amount of time. Interest and protection swirled together, muddying the lines between responsibility and want, and he had no idea if she saw him as anything other than a co-worker.

They watched the water for a while before Sage pushed his chair into motion. Soon, the first rays of sunlight started to lighten the night's darkness. "You'd gotten yourself into a situation at the bar."

"I remember him grabbing me. Then looking for my mom's ring. There are splotches of nothing. More than I care to admit."

"Nothing? As in?"

"As in, I blacked out. It used to be a couple of hours. I'd realize I was at the liquor store and had no idea how I got there. I'd have food and not know if I went out or had it delivered. Then I lost two days. Two days. I don't know what I did, where I went. The sad part is, it probably wasn't the first time, but it was the first time I'd noticed." She pulled her legs into the seat of the rocker and made herself small.

Sage nodded. "Do you want to talk to Doc Wheeler today?"

She shook her head no. "But I need to do it anyway."

They sat in the quiet of the morning. The frogs and crickets' noise lessened as the morning was born. "This is a beautiful place and view."

Sage let a sad smile spread across his face. "My mom's house. She passed."

Honor turned her head toward him. "I'm so sorry. I lost my mom just after I graduated college. She died of a brain aneurysm. No warning. One moment she was there. The next, she was gone."

Sage sighed, "My mom took the long road to glory. She died of cancer. She suffered for a long time."

Honor was silent for a moment. "It makes you wonder which is worse. The long goodbye or no goodbye." She glanced over at him. "Sorry, I didn't mean to get morbid."

"No, that's okay." Sage had talked about his mom's death with Jeremiah but no one else. "I wouldn't have wished my mom's suffering on anyone, but selfishly, we were able to talk, and I was able to understand why she lived her life the way she did."

"My mom and I were close. I told her every time we talked that I loved her. I would have cherished one more chance to let her know how much she meant to me." Honor pointed to a freighter. "Wow, that's a big boat."

"Ship," Sage automatically corrected and then chuckled. "I have a friend who has a ship. I call it a boat just to make him crazy."

"What's the difference?" Honor's voice held a hint of humor, which he'd never heard from her before.

"Well, if you ask him, it's all about size." Sage chuckled out loud, remembering the ranting lectures about the differences between ships and boats. Smoke. God, he missed being Smoke's partner. Dan Collins literally saved his life.

They were quiet for a few more moments. "He was surprised to see me."

Sage scrambled, shelving his thoughts and trying to catch up with her line of thinking. "Benedict?"

"Yeah, but his surprise wasn't in an overt way. Like in he didn't think I should be where I was type of way. I was terrified. He was startled." Honor put her toe down and pushed the rocker into motion. "I want a drink. God, I really want a drink." She rubbed her arms. It seemed to be her go-to movement to comfort herself.

Distraction time. "I can fix that. Coffee?" Sage stood up and looked at her.

Honor rolled her eyes. "Not the drink I want."

He lifted his arms in a shrug. "It's what we have. Yes or no."

"Well, if you put it that way. Yes." She stood up, and he chuckled. "Your friend has a sense of humor."

Honor pulled her t-shirt out. The words "Witness Protection Program" printed on the front were emblazoned in red on the white shirt.

Sage laughed. "That she does. She has to have a sense of humor; she's married to one of my best friends, and he's a mess. I'll go put on a shirt. Be right back." Sage made his way down the hall and grabbed a shirt from the dresser. He pulled it on and used the restroom before heading back to the kitchen.

Honor was making a pot of coffee when Sage heard a vehicle drive up. He glanced at his watch. "Did you make enough for three?"

Honor looked over her shoulder at him. "A full pot."

"Good. You're about to meet the friend Evangeline is married to."

He went to the door and waited for Beau to

climb the steps. The man had a thermal bag in his hand. "If those are hot doughnuts, I'm telling Evangeline."

"Screw you. She sent over a breakfast casserole and marching orders to get more information out of you." Beau handed him the bag and walked into the house. He stopped as soon as he saw Honor. "Ma'am."

Honor's eyes widened. Sage got it. Beau was a big guy. Taller and bulkier than Sage could ever be. His shaved head gave him a sinister look, but there wasn't a better man in the state than Beau. "Honor, this is Beau Theriot. He's the local law enforcement and my best friend growing up."

"Screw you; I'm still your best friend." Beau tossed back at Sage. "Pleasure to meet you." He looked back a Sage. "I can go if—"

"No, please. I made enough coffee for everyone," Honor spoke softly. "It's nice to meet you, Beau."

His friend melted. Sage witnessed it happen. Honor was a tiny thing, just like Evangeline. But where Evie was outgoing and bossy, Honor was quiet and timid. She evoked the desire to wrap her up and keep all the ravages of the world away from her. Sage had been through a thousand iterations of that protective impulse, and none of them were happy with the fact that Beau felt the same way. Which was ... way wrong.

"Sage?"

"Huh, what?" He'd tuned out.

"Dude, warm up the casserole. I'm starving."

"On it. Your mom and dad came over, you know," Sage said as he took the food into the kitchen.

"Believe me, my mom informed me. She says if you and the lady are here next Sunday, she's making jambalaya, and you better be there."

Sage laughed as he pressed the buttons on the microwave. "Oh, she gave me the same lecture. My mouth waters every time I think about your mom's food."

Sage arranged the table with cutlery and plates while the food warmed, and after Honor poured three cups of coffee, they sat down. The potato, cheese, bacon, and ham casserole was amazing. He tried not to watch Honor eat but was pleased when she finished about half her small serving. He and Beau laughed and talked about the days they helped Beau's dad on the Shrimper.

"Is it hard work?" Honor asked. "Shrimping?"

Her face flushed, and she dropped her eyes as

if she was embarrassed to have interrupted the conversation. Her braid was hanging over her shoulder again. She looked better today. Still pale, but better.

"It is. You work around the clock during the season. My dad's hands are so scarred from cuts from the nets that he has trouble closing his fists. But he owns his boat, leases two more, and has a good crew now, so he still works the insane hours." Beau smiled. "Working on that boat teaches a young man or woman a good work ethic. No one takes a break unless all the work is done. If y'all stick around, Sage can take you out on her. Not anytime soon, of course."

"Why?" Sage turned his attention from Honor to Beau.

Beau turned and looked at him like he was crazy. "Hurricane Kimber."

Sage sighed. "Shit. Are we in the path?"

"We are. She's a Cat One but supposed to be getting stronger."

"Mandatory evacuations?"

"No, not yet. The PPEMT is waiting to see if she's going to push east. If we're on the dirty side, I guarantee it. If we're on the clean side, probably not." The Plaquemines Parish Emergency Management Team was damn good at calling evacuations. It was a hazard of living where they lived.

"What does that mean? Dirty side and clean side?" Honor leaned forward and placed her hand on Sage's, and he glanced down at the contact. She jerked it back as if she feared she'd offended him.

Beau didn't see or at least didn't acknowledge the way she jerked back. Instead, he leaned forward and dove in with the answer. "The dirty side is the front-facing area where the hurricane is heading. In the Gulf, the main storms are to the east of the systems. It's where the hurricane pushes all the water from the gulf up onto the land because of the motion and force of the storm system. That's called the storm surge. So, if we're on the dirty side, we can expect storm surges, sometimes fifteen feet or higher, and sustained hurricane-force winds with rain. On the clean side, we'll get some flooding, feeder bands, and some pretty nasty storms with strong winds, but nothing like the dirty side." Beau explained as he used his hands to show her what he meant.

"We'll know in another twenty-four hours. She's not moving fast, but she's not gaining as much strength because of a low front that just pushed through Texas." Beau finished his coffee.

"When are you going to start working out and running with me?" he asked Sage as he stood up from the table, taking his plate and cup to the sink.

Sage winked at Honor. "When hell freezes over. You run too far."

Beau cracked a roll of laughter through the room. "Excuses, excuses. All right, I'm heading back to help Evie wrangle lil Sage and Selene. We're going to do hurricane cleanup tonight after I get off duty. Do you need anything?"

Sage shook his head. "No, I'll clean up anything that can be used as a projectile and move the truck to avoid any flood waters. Call me if we have mandatory evacuations."

"Will do. With that whole-house generator you have installed, we may all end up here with you."

"And you'd be welcome." He'd take in all the Theriots in a heartbeat.

"Good to know. Honor, it was nice to meet you." Beau dipped his head a little.

She nodded and smiled from where she sat at the kitchen table. "Later." Beau lifted a hand and headed down the stairs. Once he was gone, she looked at Sage and noted, "He's nice. They named their boy after you?"

"Yeah. Salt of the earth type people. His mom

and dad practically adopted me and took care of my younger brothers. Especially when Gus went off on a bad binge. Gus couldn't stand any of them, though."

"The Theriots? Why? Because they took care of you?"

Sage snorted. "No, because they're black. Gus was a racist asshole who thought people of color were below him." Sage shook his head. "The pigment of a person's skin doesn't determine jack shit. G-Gus is f-filth. *S-shit*."

He felt Honor move up beside him. "I'm so sorry. I didn't mean to upset you."

He held up a hand, and she turned to leave. He dropped it on her shoulder, staying her but continued to stare down at the floor as he drew in lungsful of air. Gus was a hateful person, and the Theriots were full of love. He'd seen evil, and it had nothing to do with the color of a person's skin. Gus's hate was just another reason he despised the man. The world was full of evil on small and large scales. He'd seen both and knew there was so much to do to make the world safe for everyone. Honor moved slightly, and he tried to reassure her. "N-not you." He squeezed her shoulder gently.

"Your Gus isn't a nice man."

Sage laughed. *Not my Gus, and that is the understatement of the century.*

Honor moved again, and Sage realized he still had his hand on her shoulder. He squeezed her thin shoulder again and removed the contact. Honor walked back to the table and sat down, picking up her fork and eating some more of the casserole. "The hurricane, that doesn't scare you?"

Sage grabbed the coffee pot and poured more into both of their cups. "Sometimes. This is a C-Cat One." He drew a deep breath. "You get used to them. Cat One is just a bit m-more than a bad thunderstorm. Longer, sustained winds."

Honor nodded and took another small bite. "I'm afraid of thunderstorms. I used to hide under my blankets growing up. My mom would tell me it was God bowling in the heavens."

Sage felt his eyebrows raise. "Did you believe her?"

As Honor laughed, her eyes twinkled, and her cheeks flushed. "Until I was ten and science shattered my hope."

Sage laughed with her, staring at her as she picked at the casserole. That muddled mixture of protection and attraction was there again at the surface of his thoughts. Really it was never far away. Every time she crossed his path, he felt something. Something about her presence. She was pretty, but it was more than that. He wanted to reach out for her hand, feeling both a need to take care of her as well as affection. Affection. Look at him using the big words again. Go him.

He took a drink of his coffee. "After breakfast, I'll call Jeremiah. I don't know how long we'll be here, but ..." He modulated his words carefully and was thankful he was speaking clearly. Not correctly. Clearly. That was something his speech therapist had stressed. He spoke correctly, and it was the clarity they were focusing on. Clarity could be fine-tuned. He wasn't broken. He had never been.

"I'd like that. I'm sorry I'm taking so long."

Sage lifted his coffee. "I'm enjoying the company. Take your time."

They visited for about a half hour until all the casserole on her plate was gone. Sage tried to belay her fears about the storm in the Gulf. He'd learned to prepare for the worst and hope for the best. While the tracking models were good, there was always a wobble at landfall. If they were in the cone and the storm wasn't well east of them, he'd get them out. Although the highways would be clogged when evacuation orders were given. People had learned the hard way to get out before it was too late.

Sage made his way to the office, closed the lids on the computers, picked up his phone, and called Jeremiah. He gave Honor the phone, and while she went out onto the porch and sat down on the chair, Sage headed for the shower. Jeremiah would take forever. He always did.

10

Honor sat in a chair and watched as Sage picked up things from under the house. He'd taken off his shirt, and with the load of problems she had in her bucket, she shouldn't be staring at the man, but she was. He was gorgeous. His muscles rippled as he worked, and his jeans hung low on his hips. His powerful thighs filled out the material, leaving no doubt about just how strong the man was. When Sage turned her way, she made a show of looking elsewhere. That time, she glanced at the cement pilings that the house stood on. "Why is that one different?"

There seemed to be a block of cement at the

corner of the house around a particularly large pillar.

"Emergency egress." Sage stopped what he was doing and rolled his shoulders. Not that she noticed. Okay, she noticed. Honor forced herself to attend to what he was saying. "For day-to-day use, there are the front and back stairs, but in my line of work, it pays to have a way out of the house that no one can readily see. There's a movable panel under my desk in the library. Inside this piling, there are iron rungs that you can climb down. The bricks at the bottom release, and the door swings open. He walked over and slipped his hand inside the top block. She watched as his muscles bulged, and something clicked. The side of the brick block swung out. Sage opened the door, and she could see the bottom rungs of the ladder. "It's out of view from anyone watching the front or rear steps." He swung the panel of bricks back into place.

"I thought you were Dom Ops." She blinked at Sage. "An investigator, maybe?"

Sage chuckled. "No. I've never worked Dom Ops. I was on a Thorn team until recently."

Honor blinked at that news. "Wow." The teams weren't talked about, but Honor knew they existed. They were masked at the highest level. She'd never met anyone with that high of clearance before, and she had one of the highest. Or used to, anyway.

"That's impressive."

"And antiquated already. The teams no longer exist."

"What are you doing now with Guardian?"

"Whatever I'm told." Sage laughed. "I'll learn a new skill or take on work as they see fit. I owe Guardian for so much. I don't care what they want me to do."

"God, I know that feeling." She sighed and closed her eyes. She'd fucked up and might never be able to work with Guardian again. It was a loss she would grieve. A scrape across from her popped her eyes open. Sage moved one of the last cement bricks under the house to the back of his truck.

"Are you going somewhere?" Honor asked as Sage got into his truck.

"Nope. I'm moving this up the embankment. The river will probably come out of its banks. The truck will be safer up there. I'll be right back." Sage shut the door and started his shiny black Escalade. She watched until he was out of view and then closed her eyes, soaking in the warmth and the quiet. The soft sounds of the river behind her and the warmth of the summer heat were tranquil and relaxing, but she felt jittery.

"Ready to go back upstairs, or would you like to go for a walk?" Sage asked as he brushed off his hands and headed her way. He'd put his t-shirt back on.

"A short one?" She was feeling restless, but her energy level wasn't great. She'd eaten small amounts and was drinking tons of water. She couldn't seem to keep herself hydrated.

"Let's go." He offered her a hand to help her out of the chair. She accepted it, and when he didn't release it right away, she was surprised. "Is this okay?" Sage asked as he squeezed her hand.

"Yes." She didn't know what else to say. Lord, she was so eloquent, wasn't she? They walked down the long gravel drive toward the mailbox on a pole by the main road. She glanced at him. He really should be on television. She could imagine him in a drama, saving the day and having hundreds of women following him like love-sick puppies.

"What are you thinking about?" Sage asked.

She answered honestly, "What kind of movie star you should be."

He turned to look at her and laughed, "Excuse me?"

"I think you'd be a drama star. Saving the woman from exploding buildings and riding away into the sunset."

He snorted. "I am not movie star material."

She shrugged. "You asked what I was thinking." He was so damn attractive and nice. Through the long periods at night when she couldn't sleep, she'd imagined all kinds of scenarios where they'd date or ... do more intimate things. Yes, she'd imagined what it would be like to have sex with Sage. She'd seen how other men treated their women, and she wanted that type of relationship. Not what Dean had given her. God, she felt used and filthy thinking back at how desperate she'd been to do whatever Dean had wanted her to do.

Still, none of her daydreams about her new knight in shining armor were based in reality. Sage was doing a job. Although holding her hand wasn't part of the job, was it?

"I can call Jewell and Zane and tell them we need to leave if you want." Sage opened the mailbox and checked it. He closed it, and they turned back toward the house, still holding hands.

She glanced at the brilliant blue sky. "Would you leave if I wasn't here?"

"No." He shook his head. "It's still expected only to be a Cat Two. I'd stay even if it were a direct hit. The last time I checked the weather, landfall was east of us. Even when it wobbles, we'll be good." Sage shrugged. "But we can lock up and drive north if it would make you more comfortable."

Honor stopped walking and stared at the river past the house. "I'm scared of the hurricane, but I'm more scared to leave here."

"Why?" Sage turned to face her.

She shuddered at the thought of leaving that comfortable pocket of support. Of leaving the man who had pulled her out of a floundering pile of crap and helped her stand back up. Yeah, of all the things she was afraid of, losing her connection to Sage topped the charts, and that was stupid because until he held her hand on that walk, she was damn sure the admiration was all one-sided. Yet holding his hand, her mind eased. His grasp seemed to ward off all the negative feelings and worries. His power wrapped around her with that simple touch. He was an invisible shield that buffeted the inner turmoil that plagued her.

But the other factors were legitimate, and she listed them, "Because when I do, I'm going to have to face what I've done. I'm going to have to do it alone, without you. I'm going to have to fight this constant yearning for a drink by myself. You've spoiled me."

"You deserved to be spoiled. You took the weight of the world on your shoulders." Sage moved toward the river, and she walked with him so she wouldn't have to lose their shared connection. "No matter what happens with Guardian about the security breach, you don't have to face it alone."

She walked with him for a moment as she processed that thought. "I know Dr. Wheeler will help." Unless she was fired, then she'd have to find someone else. But who? She wouldn't have insurance. "God, what a mess I made."

They stopped and stared at the water. "You're cleaning it up." Sage squeezed her hand. "I don't know what the future holds, but if you ever need to talk, I'll always be here for you."

She glanced over at him. "Sooner or later, I'll have to stand on my own two feet."

Sage nodded. "Nothing says you can't have someone hold your hand while you make that stand." He smiled at her. "We should go inside before you get a sunburn."

Honor nodded and strolled back to the house with him. At the steps, he let go of her hand and followed her up the stairs. She closed her hand, looking for the warmth and comfort he'd given her. Was it friendship, platonic support to a person down on their luck, or like her, did he want more? She didn't know.

"I'll grab the phone. It's almost time for your call with Jeremiah." Sage moved through to the office while Honor sat on the couch and stared at her nails. She'd trimmed and filed them. They weren't the broken, dirty nails she had last week, and she wasn't the broken, dirty woman she was then. Granted, she had a long, long way to go to deal with her alcohol problem, but she was clear-headed for the first time since the Siege.

She took the phone when Sage handed it to her and held it to her ear. "Hello?"

"Hi, how are you doing today?" Jeremiah asked, his tone light and carefree.

She watched Sage go back to his room and close the door. He always gave her privacy to talk with Dr. Wheeler. "I'm confused."

"About what?"

She was quiet for a long time. "If I had a crush on Sage, what would you say about it?"

That time, Dr. Wheeler paused. "I'd ask you if you thought that crush was based on anything other than him rescuing you from the darkest place you've ever existed."

Well, she'd asked, hadn't she? Honor sighed. "Maybe that's part of it."

"But not all of it."

"I don't think so. He's nice to me."

"Men aren't generally nice to you?" he asked.

She snorted. "The people I worked with were."

"But not other men? Why do you think they weren't nice to you?"

"I'm not a pretty woman. I'm a computer nerd, and I'm fat. Or I was," she amended. "The only good thing about being drunk was I didn't care about eating."

"Was that the only good thing?"

She sighed and stared out the window. "No, not feeling was great. The numbness that stopped the pain of what I'd done. I miss it, and I want it back. Really bad."

"I won't pull any punches. That craving may never go completely away. It's a long road, Honor. The numbness you were looking for, we'll get back to that before we end the call, but tell me, who said you weren't pretty?"

Honor blinked. "What?"

"Who said you weren't pretty? Name one person."

"Dean."

"Ah, the man who manipulated and used you. Any others?"

Honor shook her head. "Kids growing up. When you're made fun of all your life, you learn to deal with the truth."

"Huh." She heard paper rustling in the background. "When was the last time someone made fun of you?"

She sighed. "Dean."

"Are we starting to see a pattern here?" Dr. Wheeler asked.

"Maybe," she admitted.

There was a low chuckle at the other end of the line. "To answer your question about liking Sage, I'll say this ... He's a good man. Liking him is easy. But maybe you should focus on getting better now. Give yourself time and the grace to work on yourself for a while."

"Does that mean I can't find him attractive?" Honor deflated.

"No. Not at all, but I'm cautioning you that any relationship at this point will take your focus away from working on yourself."

"Have you met Sage? The man who calls you and puts the phone in my hand every morning?"

There was a chuff of laughter. "Noted. Consider what I said."

"And if I still want to pursue a relationship with him?" Because God, she really liked him.

"You're an adult. He's an adult." Jeremiah commented. "I'd caution against it at this time, however."

"Okay, great. I get that you want me to focus on myself. I'm probably reading too much into the way I feel. Ugggh. Seriously, I'm so confused. What if he doesn't feel the same?"

Jeremiah sighed, "Oh, the earth will open up and swallow you."

Honor laughed hard and unexpectedly. She shook her head. "You need help."

"Yeah, my wife tells me that all the time. Look, Honor, you like Sage. Maybe he likes you, too. Maybe he doesn't. You're both adults. You'll figure it out, but don't let a relationship detract from the work at hand, which is your sobriety. Now, let's circle back to Dean ..."

SAGE WAITED until he knew Honor was asleep. After a session with Jeremiah, she was drained. She usually made her way back to her room and slept, and today was no exception. Still, he took the phone out onto the porch and closed the door for privacy as Jeremiah had requested in a text after Honor's session.

"Dr. Wheeler."

"She's asleep. I can talk. What's wrong?"

Jeremiah sighed. "I can't go into specifics about what Honor and I talked about, but I want to caution you that in the role you're currently in, well, it's easy for a person to get caught up in transference."

Sage looked at the wood decking under his boots. "Jeremiah, I have no idea what you're talking about. I'm a hick from Louisiana. Spell it out."

Jeremiah sighed, "She's vulnerable."

"No shit." Sage spit the words out. "She's also been hurt by a bastard who used her, is terrified of what Guardian will do about her screw-up, and is going through alcohol withdrawal. All of that is because of one person. I want to find that bastard Benedict and pound him into the ground. She deserves better. No one has the right to hurt that woman, and I'm going to make damn sure it doesn't happen again."

There was silence for a moment. "Ah. Okay."

"What? What does that mean?" Sage laughed. "Dude, are you messing with my head just for fun?"

"Nope. I'm not. I just wanted to know where you stood."

"On what issue?" Sage lifted his hand in the air. "Doc, you're not making sense."

"I think I am."

"Whatever, so there's nothing that I need to worry about? She's working with you, right?"

"She is. No worries. My next patient is here. We'll talk later." Jeremiah disconnected.

Sage looked at his phone and then at the river. "What the hell was that about?" His phone vibrated in his hand, and he answered it.

"Yo."

"Are you evacuating?" Zane's voice popped across the connection.

Sage looked out at the brilliant blue sky and calm river. "No. We're good here. I have a generator, and with this phone, I'll have a connection when the cell towers go out."

"How do you know the cell towers will go out?"

"Because they always do. The satellite phone will be our connection to you after the storm passes or between feeder bands. I'm not sure if we can get a signal through when the storm is overhead."

"Huh. Hold on a minute. Jewell, what are the chances of using a satphone during a hurricane?"

"Iridium-based phones have a strong signal and may get through. It could be touch and go," Sage heard Jewell answer in a distracted type of way.

"Okay, so we might have periods of time where we can't be in contact. You stay put and keep yourself and Honor high and dry."

"Will do. Although Honor's worried about the storm, she's willing to stick it out with me. I've been through enough hurricanes to know this isn't going to be that bad."

"A Cat Two with a possibility of strengthening to a Cat Three isn't that bad?"

"No, perhaps I chose my words incorrectly. The wind and rain are destructive but not bad enough to head north."

"All right, we'll have to trust your judgment on that. I was just checking in. How's Honor doing?"

Sage sat down on one of the rockers. "She's getting better, but she's terrified of what's going to happen with Guardian. She didn't tell me that, but I can tell."

"Yeah, so far, it's been radio-silent from the brass. I'm sure they want all the details before they make a final decision."

"What can happen?"

Zane let out a long breath. "Man, I'm not sure. She messed up. The reasons why are compelling, but she covered up a security breach. That's up there on the 'oh shit' list." He heard Zane close a door behind him.

"Give me a ballpark, Zane."

"Depending on the situation, it could range from a reprimand to termination to jail time."

"Fuck." Sage dropped his head back. "She can't go to jail for this."

"It isn't my call. I'll do everything I can to plead her side of the case, and so will Jewell. I don't think it'll go that far, but a lot depends on what we find on her systems."

"When will that be done?"

"Tomorrow latest," Zane answered.

"This phone will be on, and I'll be waiting for an update." Sage sighed. "She's a good person caught in a shit situation."

"I know," Zane agreed. "Take care of her."

"I plan on it." Sage hung up and rocked as he stared sightlessly toward the water. Honor had become important in his life. Quickly. That should have bothered him, but it didn't. Life was full of hard punches. Meeting Honor had been more like a drawn-out, slow-motion fist flying his way. He could see it coming, he knew it would smack him upside the head, but he damn sure didn't want to move.

He shook his head. Guardian would do what was right. They always did. He had to believe they would see what he saw. Honor was worth fighting for.

11

Jewell stared at the screen. There. It had taken her three days to find it. But there it was. "I see it," she whispered.

"Where?" Zane rolled forward from his desk.

"Here. I can see where they came into the system." She pointed to the lines of code she was referencing. "Why didn't I see it then?"

"Because you weren't looking for it?"

Jewell shook her head. "No, I was." She'd gone through the system with a fine-tooth comb. Or she'd thought she had.

"Then I'd go with you didn't have the knowledge or experience you have now. If you had, you would have found it. I don't doubt it for a moment." Zane handed her a bottle of water. She took it out of routine and opened it, downing half. "I can see what they accessed and what she blocked."

"Did they get anything other than the information they acted on?"

"No. It was all communications that weren't shielded. We don't have that any longer. Everything they knew was pieced together. They had to be in the system for a while. Listening and watching without us knowing." Jewell drank the rest of her water. She scrolled through lines of data until she saw what Honor had been talking about. "Here. This is where they tried to burrow in further. Why would they wait?"

"Because they wanted to ensure the information they'd accessed was correct. Once the events started happening, they confirmed the data," Zane explained.

Yeah. That would be the reason. Jewell stared at what had happened. The cloned copy of the data was ancient by computer standards, and she'd had to make a sleigh for the old drive so her new computers could work with the old hardware with the ancient information. "She was good." Jewell focused on the patch that Honor had created and then moved the visual of the code to screens Zane could see. "See here. She outmaneuvered her own program."

Zane leaned over. "Yeah, okay. If you say so."

Jewell rolled her eyes. "I say so. What happened that night could have been so much worse. So much worse. She saved the company."

"From her own program."

"That was stolen."

"We'll let the powers-that-be determine what's going to happen to her. But for now, we need to get back to her computers so we can get her out of limbo. I know we had to validate what she said, but with the amount of time it's taken to do that, I'm sure she's freaking out." Zane dropped his arm over her shoulder. "But before we go any further, we need to take a break for lunch."

Jewell twisted so she could see her husband. "Pizza?"

He smiled. "Sure. I'll fire up the pizza oven."

"Perfect. I'm going to put this information into a memo and send it to Jason."

"Good idea. Don't take too long, or I'll take all the pepperoni," Zane said as he left the office and started down the ramp to the kitchen. Jewell spun on her chair in a three-sixty. She loved her cave, but she loved Zane more than anything in the world. Even her computers. She glanced at the screens filled with code. She wished Honor had someone like Zane because the future could be hard for her, depending on what Jason determined about the unreported security breach.

HONOR LISTENED to the wind howling through the hurricane shutters. The rain pelted the outside of the house, hitting the siding so hard it sounded like someone knocking on the sides of the structure. She pulled the fur blanket around her.

"Starting to come onto shore," Sage said as he came in from the kitchen with a bowl of popcorn. "Have you picked a movie?"

Honor shook her head. "No." *God, she wanted a drink. A big one. A whole fucking bottle.* She rubbed her arms and sighed. "You pick. It's your turn."

Sage did a double take at her before grabbing the remote off the coffee table and turning the power on the television. "Comedy or drama?"

"I think there's enough drama outside." Honor jumped when a clap of thunder rumbled the floor under her. "We're on the clean side, right?"

"We are. Nothing to worry about," Sage said as he sat beside her and put the popcorn on her lap.

Another clap of thunder shook the house. "Nothing to worry about."

"Nothing at all." Sage pushed the right buttons, and a black-and-white comedy came on the set.

"Abbot and Costello." She laughed and tried to focus on the screen. But as she grabbed a few kernels of corn and watched the opening credit, a brilliant flash followed by a sonic boom shook the house. Honor screamed and ducked under the fur blanket. *Holy shit! We're going to die.* Good God, she'd gone through withdrawal for nothing.

"Hey, are you okay?" Sage tapped the blanket she was cowering under.

"No," because, *obviously,* she wasn't.

Sage tugged on the blanket. "You do realize a piece of fabric won't save you, right?"

She whipped the fake fur off her. "Why? You couldn't let me believe it until the storm was over. Hey, what happened to the lights?" Honor heard an engine start in between the waves of wind pummeling the house. The lights flickered back on.

"Generator. It runs on propane. We have enough to power the house for about two weeks."

Sage pointed the remote at the television and turned it off. Another clap of thunder made her jump. "You weren't joking about being afraid of thunderstorms, were you?"

"*Why* would I joke?" Honor sighed and looked at the floor. "Oh, man. I'm sorry." The popcorn bowl was upended and on the floor. She scurried to pick up the mess.

He bent down at the same time, and their faces were less than an inch apart. Honor froze. Sage smiled and then moved to grab the bowl. She knew her face was turning morbidly red with embarrassment. Her coloring had always given away when she was flustered. She wished she hadn't braided her hair and that she could hide behind it. Man, that and a bottle of vodka. Hell, she'd drink anything right now. Cough medicine ... anything. She put a handful of popcorn back in the bowl.

Another pop of lightning flashed, and almost immediately, thunder shook the house. Honor jumped backward, knocking the bowl on its side again.

Sage shook his head. "I'll get this. You can hide in the corner."

"Yeah, good idea." Honor scooted back up into

the couch and pulled the blanket over her. Every time the thunder rumbled, she'd jump underneath the blanket.

She felt Sage sit down beside her. "Come here." His arm was behind her back, and he urged her toward him. The loud clap of thunder outside sealed the deal. She pushed next to him and pulled the blanket with her, dipping under it when another roll of thunder vibrated the structure.

"How long will this last?"

"What, this? Not long. It won't get bad until the bigger feeder bands reach us."

Honor lifted her head and stared at the man holding her. "What?"

"This is the front edge of the storm. We're safe. The house is well grounded, we have generator power, and we're built above any storm surge."

Oh, merciful bits of dirty data ... no ... "You mean it gets worse?"

Sage tried not to smile but ended up laughing. "Just a bit."

"Great." She pulled the blanket over her head again. "I want alcohol. A whole bottle. Any kind."

"Sorry, don't have any. What did you do for Guardian?" Sage asked as he adjusted on the couch, leaning to his side and pulling her with him.

Honor shoved the thought of alcohol as far away as she could, which wasn't far, and moved, staying connected to the man she prayed was as good at fighting thunderstorms as he was bikers and Russian mobsters. She pulled the blanket down to talk. "At first, I did whatever I was assigned to do. When you're a young operator, Jewell and other senior operators will put you through your paces. We all took turns doing missions for overseas teams, running satellite coverage, communications, that type of thing. Eventually, we extended our reach into Dom Ops. When they have an operation going on, we're there to expedite anything that needs to be handled. I was promoted to night shift supervisor about four years ago, and now I mostly work on security, stabilizing our platform as it grows. We only use proprietary programs. Ones that were developed at Guardian."

"Did you help develop them?"

"I have, yes."

"Is it hard?"

She shook her head, feeling him breathing under her. "It's the most exciting thing in the world. Doing things that no one else has done is mesmerizing. Defeating threats that have brought others to their knees gives you such a charge. Sometimes it's tedious, don't get me wrong, but knowing you're part of something like Guardian, that your contributions make a difference in the mission that they're doing. It's so ... I don't know, empowering, I guess."

"Have you always been good with computers?"

She jumped and edged closer when a tremendous clash of thunder rumbled through the house. "Yes. They make sense." *Unlike people.*

Sage chuckled. "You say that like other things don't."

"To you, they might. I've been told I'm naïve." *And fat and disgusting.* Dean's voice ripped through her thoughts. She drew a breath and remembered what Jeremiah had said yesterday.

"There's nothing wrong with that."

"There is when it allows others to take advantage of you." Dean wasn't the only person to use her to get what they needed. In college, she'd helped others because she thought they were friends. They were until they'd gotten what they wanted or needed, and boom, she was alone again. "You'd think I'd learn."

"Trusting people isn't a bad thing." Sage rubbed his hand up and down her arm when another clap of thunder sounded.

She sighed and relaxed into him. "I'll agree to disagree with you." She changed the subject. "Dr. Wheeler is nice until he isn't."

Sage snorted. "Those last minutes when you've got it all sorted out, and then he asks a couple of questions that have you relooking at everything."

She leaned up a bit. "Yes. That. Then you think about nothing but those questions. You pick through everything looking for an answer, think you have it, and he changes the premise again."

Sage tossed his head back and laughed. "You don't know how many times I cussed him under my breath. But damn it, having him beside you when you poke around at all that mess helps. God, it really helps."

"Hopefully." Right now, she'd withhold judgment. She had hour-long sessions with him every day. She might have a session with him tomorrow. If she lived long enough. She jumped at a clap of thunder. The storm was raging outside, and sometimes it seemed like the thunder was one continuous vibration. Sage continued to rhythmically rub her arm. She relaxed into him.

"Do you think Beau is okay?" He told them last night that he had to work during the storm. All the deputies did, or so he said. He'd stopped by after work to make sure they didn't need anything. He was taking his family to Evangeline's parent's house, which was farther inland. Beau's parents were riding out the storm and had the shrimpers moved to a safer harbor. Honor liked Beau. She hadn't met Evangeline yet, but Beau said it was because they were working on hurricane prep. She'd be around sooner rather than later.

"Yeah, they'll pull the deputies off the road once the weather gets bad."

"Like now," Honor added.

"Like a couple of hours from now. Once the wind reaches a certain level, they're told to return to the station. The Cajun Navy is probably staged there, too."

"The what?"

"A bunch of volunteers who go out after the worst of the storm is over and rescue people stranded by high water, had their houses damaged, or maybe were washed out of their homes. They bring their shallow hulled boats that can maneuver in flood waters and go to places the police and fire-rescue personnel can't reach."

"How do they know where to go?" She looked up at him.

"The guys I know use ham radios. Cell phones aren't much good once the towers go down. Unless you have a satellite phone like I do."

"Sounds ..." *Stupid, scary, ridiculously heroic ...* "dangerous."

"They're dedicated and know how to get their boats through the debris in the shallow waters. Some of them use the boats for fishing or to go gator hunting in the swamp."

"Fishing for alligators?"

"Fishing? No, not really. It's more like a death wrangle and rifle type thing."

"I'm sorry, that sounds absolutely stupid. What have the alligators done to them?"

Sage shrugged. "It controls the population."

Honor grunted, "I'm rooting for the alligators," which caused Sage to laugh. She liked the sound of his laughter. It was rich and deep and filled her ear that was pressed against his chest.

They were quiet for a while before Honor asked a question that had been on her mind for some time, "I wonder why Jewell hasn't called. It shouldn't have taken this long, even if she's busy with other work."

"I don't know. How long does it take to do a forensic sweep of your computers?" Sage continued to run his hand up and down her arm. Honor loved the sensation of his warm skin against hers. It had been so long since she'd had any human interaction at that level. A reassuring touch was so much more than a gesture.

"It depends on what she finds. I know my primary is pristine. The laptops? Who knows. I told you I blacked out. I could have gone to Hubby Porn and Play dot com or something."

Sage's laughter was louder than the thunder outside, and her entire body vibrated in time with his laughs. "Oh, my God, warn a guy, will you?" He tried to stop laughing but couldn't.

She elbowed up. "What, it's okay for guys to visit porn sites but not women?"

"I didn't say that. I just never expected those words to come out of your mouth." Sage settled back into his corner, still chuckling, and she dropped back onto his chest.

"Why?"

"Because you're a tiny, cute, shy, and timid woman. Hubby Porn and Play dot com was the last thing I expected you to say."

"I'm none of those things, actually. Well, maybe timid, but none of the others."

Sage twisted so he could see her. "Agree to disagree."

"About what?"

"I call it as I see it. To me, you are tiny and very cute, and I see your shyness, or perhaps it's a fear that you cloak as shyness. I see you, Honor, and I believe I see the real you. I've seen you at your rock bottom, and I've watched you claw back up to the surface. I know you're still fighting the desire for alcohol, and that makes you strong. I get glimpses of your humor and your wit. I like you for you, so you can either accept it or not. But that's what I see."

Honor tipped her head back. "Wow, that was a speech and a half. Do you make all the women in your life feel this good?"

Sage lifted an eyebrow. "Being with you on this couch, holding you, is something I haven't done in ..." He sighed and shook his head, "years."

"I know that feeling," she admitted. "I've only dated a couple of times after Dean. Nothing that went anywhere." Instead, she found comfort in food and her computers. Hell, she didn't even have a cat or houseplants because she spent most of her time at Guardian.

"I was in the military and usually deployed. Then the injury happened. It was weird. Maybe a week after the accident, I just started stuttering. Jeremiah thinks I saw something or someone said something that may have triggered the issue. Anyway, my stuttering prevented me from talking to anyone except a very few close friends. I found out it was because I trusted them implicitly. I still stuttered, but not as much." He shrugged. "Sometimes a person is destined to wait for the right one to come along."

Honor chuckled. "Sounds like something my mom would have said."

"My mom did say it." Sage adjusted and put his feet up on the couch. "Right after she asked if I had a girlfriend."

Honor moved and wiggled up a bit on his chest. A loud rush of wind against the house made the structure creak, and Honor bolted into a sitting position.

"Relax. It's just the wind."

She gaped at him. "Or a flipping tornado."

"No, you'd know if it was a tornado. They sound like a freight train heading your way."

Honor squeaked as the breath squeezed in her chest. "There are tornados, too?"

Sage's brow furrowed as he pulled her back down. "There are, but mostly inland. Not so much around here. I saw one in South Dakota. It was dancing over the plains, just doing its thing. There was this massive storm front, and it was this dark blue, almost black cloud bank as far as you could see. The tail of the tornado just dipped out of the clouds and slowly swayed toward the ground. The initial column was pure white and pristine. Then as it got closer to the ground, you could see the spin of the air around the funnel. You could see the dirt and debris sucked upward into the cone, turning it dark. What didn't go up in the funnel you could see circling around the outside. I've never seen anything with that much raw power. I know a hurricane has power, but a hurricane is so big that you don't see that focused pinpoint of impact, you know?"

Honor stared up at him. "You're poetic. Do you know that? You made a tornado sound majestic."

Sage shrugged. "When you can't talk easily, you think. I've done a lot of thinking."

"I'm happy you're talking to me." She'd tipped her head up and gazed up at him. He looked down at her. Those beautiful brown eyes of his stared back at her, and she wanted him to kiss her. She wanted to feel his lips on hers. God help her; she wanted to feel his arms tighten around her, protecting her. Sage licked his lips, and she watched, fixated on the sensuality of the moment.

He leaned down slowly. Dear heavens, so slowly. When his lips touched hers, she sighed and melted into his body. He licked her bottom lip, and she opened her mouth for him. The taste of him exploded on her tongue, his scent filled her senses, and her lips tingled from his touch. The kiss was slow, sensual, hot, and far, far too short.

Sage lifted away from her and stared down at her. "I don't want to take advantage of you."

Honor blinked up at him, not following. "What? How?"

"You're not a hundred percent."

Oh. Honor reached up and slid her fingers through his long, silky brown hair. "I'm not. But I'm not drunk, and I'm not sick. I'm recovering, and from what Jeremiah tells me, I may always be recovering. I know what's happening here between us. I *want* what's happening."

Sage's hand reached down and moved a piece of hair that had escaped her braid. "And what happens when Jewell calls and a decision is reached?"

Honor broke eye contact and looked at his chest. "I'll face that when it happens."

"That's not what I meant." He tipped her chin up, forcing her to look at him. "When we aren't in forced proximity, would you still want me to be the one who kisses you? Am I the type of man you'd let into your life?"

Honor tried to breathe; she really did. She stared at him and asked, "Would you still want to kiss me?" Dean's words danced across her memory. He'd forced himself to make love to her. She was fat, ugly, and disgusting.

"Yes. God, yes." Sage dropped for a kiss. It was heated, deeper, and longer. She wrapped her arms around his neck. The feel of his big shoulders over her satisfied something deep inside of her. When he released her lips, he asked again, "Am I the type of man you'd let into your life?"

As he'd said, he'd been with her at the bottom and every step of the way from that moment. "You're already in my life. Please stay."

Honor held him as he moved. She opened her legs, accepting him over her. Sage might not have been with a woman recently, but that didn't mean he didn't know how to kiss or touch. The almost continuous roll of thunder was a distant background noise to the orchestrated melody Sage was playing on her body. Her shirt was pushed up and moved. The new bra was gone. His shirt was next. The feel of his chest hair against her breasts sent a shockwave straight to her core. *Oh. Yes.* His lips traveled lower, and her back arched as his lips trailed over her breast. Sensations she'd never experienced before welled in a tight, pulsing need. She held his shoulders as he worked off her jeans. "Yours. Off."

Honor was lost to the moment. She only felt need and want. The feel of him naked on top of her ignited a deeper desire. She lost herself in Sage's kiss. The feel of his body against hers and the hard length pressed against her hip. Sage rose to his knees and grabbed his jeans. He pulled out his wallet and retrieved three condoms. Opening one, he stared at her as he rolled it down his shaft. Honor watched him. His body was stunning and muscled, and his cock was hard and heavy in his hand. "Are you sure?"

She lifted her eyes to the man above her. "Yes." The answer was definite.

He lifted her and sat on the couch, pulling her

over his lap. Honor was confused at first. She'd never had sex in any position except on her back.

Sage pulled her into him and tipped his head back, kissing her. He cupped her breasts with his hands and rolled the nipples lightly between his fingers, making her gasp at the sensation. Sage centered his cock under her. "Whenever you're ready." He pulled her down for another kiss, one hand holding his shaft and the other gently rolling her nipple. Honor lowered as they kissed. She groaned when the cap of his shaft entered her. Sage never stopped kissing her, stimulating her. She moved up and down, slowly accepting his cock inside her until she was sitting on his lap with him completely inside her.

Sage held her hips, lifting her about six inches. He thrust into her and retreated. The slow upward scrape of his cock against the inside of her core set off little explosions of sensation. She closed her eyes and arched her back, holding onto his shoulders. Her eyes popped open when she felt his fingers at the apex of her sex. The pressure and rubbing spiked pleasure through her in a way she'd never experienced. "Sage!" She gasped his name. He claimed her mouth in a kiss and quickened his pace. A physical shock clamped her core against him, and the clenching rhythm continued, twisting and tightening in shots of pleasure and pain that exploded into a starburst of sensation.

Honor clutched Sage's shoulders and held on as he finished. Completely drained, she dropped forward, his cock still inside her. Sage enfolded her in his arms and draped the fake fur blanket over them. The storm raged outside. Honor didn't care. If she died tonight, she'd die happy.

12

Jewell chewed on a piece of toast as she stared at her monitor. "Well, okay, then." She chuckled and shook her head at one of the websites that Honor had visited. She had her own hubby porn in real life, so who was she to judge.

"What's that?" Zane asked from his desk.

"Nothing." Jewell continued to check the browser history of Honor's laptop. It was the first step and usually the most boring, but Honor hadn't been careful with that computer recently. She clicked on a messenger app and waited for the page to populate.

Jewell stuck the toast between her teeth and used the passwords Honor had given her to open her accounts. Careless, using the same password for public apps. But then again, Honor hadn't been herself lately.

Letting it populate, Jewell spun around. "How bad is the hurricane?"

"It's a Cat Two, so bad, but not as bad as the weather people wanted it to be." Zane rolled his eyes.

"Right? It's like they're banking on a disaster to boost their ratings." Jewell glanced up at the television above Zane's desk. The bright orange rain jackets were the focal point of the reporting. "They didn't leave?" She watched the clips of the worst of the weather.

"No. Sage said they were safe, and he wasn't worried." Zane leaned back in his chair and looked up, shaking his head as he talked to the monitor. "Idiots. Get out of the rain."

"Then it wouldn't be as dramatic." Jewell finished her toast and dusted off her hands. "All right, back to browser history."

"When you finish that, we have a metric shit-ton of priority requests."

"What's Ethan doing?" Jewell got up and walked over to where the computer queue of tasks was accumulating.

"Everything you're not in the upper classification. We need to have others working the lesser tasks." Zane pulled her down into his chair. "Toast isn't a nutritious breakfast."

"But it's good, and I had peanut butter on the first piece. I'll have something green for lunch." She kissed his nose and stood up.

"I'll guarantee it," Zane said as she sat back down in her chair. She turned around and started reading. Jewell leaned forward and scrolled ... and scrolled. "Well, I found out how the Bratva knew where she was. Hell, Honor stayed on this messaging app way too long. A child with no computer skills would have been able to track her if they wanted."

Jewell went to the menu and hit print. The printer started spewing out sheets of paper as she copied the text and placed it in another file. She then started dissecting the chat room. It was one she hadn't seen before.

Zane stood at the printer and read the conversation. "How would she know to contact him on this chat forum?"

"It was added to this computer years ago. Right before she started working with us. Check the date." Jewell threw the information she was looking at onto an overhead monitor where Zane could see it. She toggled the mouse by the date she was talking about. "I didn't go too far back. What is the first chat?"

"Um ... hold on." Zane pulled the last piece of paper from the printer. "Someone called Dizzy Dean. Wow. He's a tool."

"Why?" Jewell swiveled around.

"Listen to this. *I'll be there at nine. Be showered and ready. I'll fuck you, but I have to leave after.*"

Jewell blinked and then turned slowly back to the computer. "Honor, I'm so sorry. No one should have to have their past sifted through like this."

"Oh, it gets worse. God, I want to deck this guy. No one should treat another human like this." Zane shook his head. He continued to flip papers. "I hate this man." He mumbled several times. Jewell couldn't agree more. Honor had hooked up with a total tool.

"Wait, here. Listen to this. This is from Honor. *You have to bring it back; you took that program without permission. You can't use it. Dean, don't do this to me.*"

Jewell sighed and dropped her head. "Did he respond?"

"Yep. He said fuck off." Zane grabbed another

piece of paper. "The next message was from him, but years later. He's been pinging her in this app since ... Yep, last year. Hey, babe, yadda, yadda, I'm a changed man, and I want to apologize. I can see you're reading the messages. I went by your apartment. You moved." Zane shuffled through the papers giving her the highlights. "After the Siege, he became demanding, threatening. Fucker told her Guardian's demise was her fault. She was the reason all the people died. If she'd come with him, they'd be alive. God, what a fucker. She read them but didn't respond."

Jewell switched screens and scrolled to last week. "The first time she replied to him was the day after *we* contacted her. "*Go fuck yourself. Bastard.* Well, good for you, Honor."

Zane nodded. "He answered, but she didn't."

"My bet is she went out for more alcohol, or she went to sleep." Jewell looked at the data. "She was online for over ten hours. That's how they found her."

"She probably passed out." Zane agreed. "But why do they want her?"

"Big question of the day. Would you ping Ethan about the background check on Mr. Dean Benedict?"

"On it," Zane said and picked up the phone that connected them to the Annex.

Jewell worked on the computer, which was old but well-made and upgraded. Another notch of respect for Honor. She knew how to keep her systems upgraded and updated. Well, with the exception of that stupid messaging app. Another monitor lit up, and she saw it out of the corner of her eye. Jewell swung over and read the message. "Jason wants a sitrep about Honor tomorrow morning."

"Then let's get the dissecting done so we have all the answers we can provide," Zane said as he gathered the printed paper. "I'll put this in the timeline with the rest of the information we've pulled."

"Rog-O." Jewell spun back to Honor's laptop. "What else do you have for me, you lovely piece of ghosted hard drive? Give up your secrets, or I'll make you walk the plank."

"If that computer answers, I'm out of here," Zane said from his desk. Jewell laughed and rubbed her hands together. Time to get busy.

∾

SAGE HELD Honor in his arms and listened to the storm raging outside. The wind was sustained as the Category Two hurricane came ashore last night. Yet his thoughts centered on Honor and the bridge they crossed while the storm raged. He didn't regret a moment of what they'd done, and he prayed she didn't either.

He hadn't been with a woman in a hell of a long time. The last time had been almost three years ago, and the disappointment that encounter had brought still lingered. No intimacy, no feelings, desolate and emotionless. A physical act with a woman he didn't know and who didn't give a shit about him. But now he was there, in this room, with Honor, and he felt something stirring within him. He stared up at the ceiling, watching the shadows dance in the pale yellowish hue of the one light that remained on in the living room. Sage liked her. Admired her strength and determination. Fighting the alcohol and learning to deal with life without the chemical assistance she'd grown addicted to had to be pure hell. And yet she was fighting.

The silence of the early morning was broken by the howl of the wind against the house, but it didn't wake her. Sage gazed down, and as he studied her, he felt a vivid reminder of what it meant to be alive, to feel something, to be connected to another person. He felt his heart fill, inviting a new sense of hope. He wanted to reach out, to touch her, and to find out if she felt the same. But he stayed still, afraid that if he moved, this moment, this feeling would be lost forever.

No matter what she said, she was beautiful. Her big blue eyes reflected her feelings. He could see into her soul when he looked into her eyes. There was no subterfuge or pretense with her. When she was hurting for a drink, he could tell, and he tried to reroute the conversation or suggest a movie or a walk. When she thought about what she'd done early in her career with Guardian, the regret rolled off her. No, the woman was an open book, and he prayed Guardian took the length of her work, the fact that the program had been stolen, and that she'd stopped further attacks into consideration. But the end game was out of their hands.

Regardless, the feeling he had right now, the contented, relaxed comfort with her, was something he wanted more of. He wanted more of Honor. She shifted beside him, and he let her resettle before he covered them with the fur blanket. As much as he wanted what was between him and Honor to stay private, he would let Jeremiah know in general terms that they'd become intimate. It was only fair to Honor. God knew he didn't want to impede her recovery or become her crutch. Like his use of sign language had become his. It allowed him not to address his issues. Useful in the beginning but a crutch at the end.

Sage tilted his head and listened. The storm was starting to subside. The lightning strikes and thunder had diminished, and the wind was ebbing as the feeder moved inland. They were still in for a long deluge as the storm meandered onto land because it was slow moving, which would cause flooding. The sustained winds, with the saturation of the rain, would bring down trees and power poles.

Mississippi and Alabama would be the worst hit. But the people who lived on the coast were tough and knew how to prepare and evacuate if necessary.

He glanced at his cell phone, noting the time. Almost seven in the morning.

"Is this where things get awkward?" Honor mumbled from beside him.

He turned and looked down at her. "God, I hope not."

She smiled, and it lit up her eyes. "I've never slept all night with anyone. I'm not sure about what to do."

Sage chuckled and wrapped her up in his arms. "Well, I haven't had a lot of experience with overnight visits before, but I'd say we say good morning, hit the shower, grab some coffee and eat some breakfast."

"Sounds perfect." A loud thud against the house made Honor jump. "What was that?"

"Could have been anything. A rock carried by the wind. It doesn't matter. The shutters will keep the windows safe."

"How bad is it outside?" Honor lifted up. Her tumble of brown hair fell to her shoulders as she squinted, looking at the front door.

"Bad enough to stay inside." Sage ran his hand up her spine, feeling the smooth expanse of her skin, and she arched a bit into his touch. He leaned down and kissed her forehead. "Care to share a shower with me?"

Honor gazed up at him. A shy smile played at the corner of her lips. "I think I'd like that."

Sage flipped the faux fur blanket off them, and

they untangled to stand up. Then he helped her off the couch, and they walked back to his bedroom. He let her use the facilities while he brushed his teeth. With a start, Sage remembered the condoms and made quick work of walking out to the living room to claim the two he'd left while he brushed his teeth. He found Honor coming out of her bedroom with a toothbrush. "Great minds?" She held the brush.

He winked at her and followed her into the bathroom. After he finished brushing his teeth, he started the shower and stepped in. The warmth of the water slithered down his back, and he dropped his head under the water. He felt rather than saw when Honor opened the door. He lifted his lids and looked at her. Her brown hair fell past her shoulders, and she had a rose hue from either excitement or embarrassment. He'd bank on the latter. She had no concept of how attractive she was. Someone had done a number on her, and he had no doubt who that bastard was.

Sage extended his hand, and she accepted it. He tugged gently, bringing her closer to him. When she stood in front of him, he wrapped her in his arms and bent to kiss her. She tasted of mint, but underneath was the flavor he'd developed an addiction to last night. He turned so she would be under the fall of water. Sage kept the kiss going, coaxing and teasing her. When she relaxed into him, the primal protector buried somewhere inside of him roared in approval. Sage couldn't agree more. He fucking loved that she was able to trust him. He'd damn sure make sure she never had to doubt that trust. Ever.

He slowly broke away from the kiss, returning for small tastes as his hand snaked out and found the soap. He lathered his hands. "Turn around."

The sudden look of surprise and concern in her eyes jarred him. "I'm going to wash your back." He leaned down and kissed her again.

"Oh." She nodded and turned away from him. Sage pushed her hair over her shoulders and used the soap to massage her shoulders, easing their tension. He grabbed the bar and worked his way down to her shoulder blades. Tracing the curve of her spine, he continued down to her waist. He circled her waist with his hands and moved to her hips. He carefully washed her ass and the top of her thighs, making the movements as sensual as possible. He lifted one leg at a time to wash the soles of her feet. When he was done, he used his hands to turn her. He started at her ankles and worked his way up her legs. At the apex of her thighs, he concentrated on her sex. Her hands landed on his shoulders, and she gripped tightly after the soap washed off. It might have had something to do with where his tongue traveled. She gasped. Her shocked vocalization bounced off the shower walls. Sage's inner protector pounded his chest again when she put her hand on the back of his head and lifted her leg over his shoulder. Yes, God, yes. He wrapped his arms around her and brought her to his mouth, wanting more of her.

Her fingers worked their way through his hair, and when he felt her thighs tremble, those fingers clenched. He devoured her as her gasps echoed around them. When he felt her go limp, he licked her thigh and kissed it before he stood up and held her in his arms.

"Oh, God. That was ... fantastic." He chuckled and rocked her from one foot to the other. She finally dropped her head back to look at him. "What about you?"

Sage dropped a kiss on her upturned lips. "That was all about you." He'd decided that while on his knees. His cock didn't agree, not in any way, shape, or form, but with Honor, Sage was willing to make the sacrifice. Hell, the sex last night broke one doozy of a dry spell for him, so his cock could shut the fuck up. Honor needed to see that he cared about her, about how she felt, and that she mattered. He didn't think she'd ever felt that way. A guess on his part but an educated one.

Honor stared up at him. "You're mad at me?"

Sage jerked his head up. "What? No, why would I be?" Honor shrugged and looked down. He put his finger under her chin and gently lifted her chin. "Why would you think that?"

"Just … in the past … never mind."

"In the past, what? I'm not mad at you. The opposite, in fact. I wanted that time to be about and for you. To show you how much you matter to me. Talk to me, please?"

She leaned against him, her forehead resting on his chest. "When he didn't like what I did, he wouldn't finish, and he'd leave. He didn't like me touching him."

Sage wrapped his arms around her. "Then he's an absolute fucking idiot. I want you to touch me whenever you want. If I'm ever upset with you, I'll tell you. I hope you'd do the same."

She looked up at him again. "I'll try. It's hard to …" She sighed, and her shoulders dropped before she whispered, "He's the only experience I've had until you. What *we've* done is ..." She stopped talking. Sage could tell she had to stop, or she'd start crying.

Sage backed her into the water and cupped the back of her head in his hand, supporting her when he asked, "Lean back." He watched as she closed her eyes and leaned back into the water. He wet her hair and grabbed the shampoo, still holding her in his grasp. "What we've done has nothing to do with him. It has to do with us. We've got a lot of roads to travel together. They might not all be smooth, but I want to go down them to find out what's at the end."

Sage massaged her scalp, and she moaned, lifting her hands to his biceps. He worked the suds through her hair and rinsed them out. When he lifted her, she collapsed against his chest. "If I'm in a dream, never wake me."

"You're not dreaming." Sage held her against him. "Let's get some breakfast, and then I'll check outside to make sure everything is standing."

Honor leaned back to look up at him. "Outside? Is it safe?"

He opened the door and grabbed a towel, handing it to her before taking one for himself. "I'm not going too far. We can open a shutter on the opposite side of the house from where the wind is coming. I have game cameras set up, but we can't use them without connectivity."

"What do you use the game cameras for?"

"I wanted to have a way to check in on the contractors working on the house. It was easy to log in to the system and see the activity."

They toweled off, and Sage wrapped the towel around his waist. He walked up behind Honor, who was drying her hair with another towel while wrapped in the one he gave her. "You're beautiful."

She lowered her eyes, and her hands stopped working with her hair. "I'm not."

Sage turned her around and lifted her chin gently. "To me, you are." He leaned down and kissed her. When they separated and she opened her eyes, he repeated. "To me, you're beautiful."

13

Honor pulled on jeans and a t-shirt before she padded into the kitchen and started a pot of coffee. Sage whistled happily as he walked past her into the living room and then into the office. A warmth tingled through her, and she smiled. Sage was indeed her knight in shining armor. Her knight. She sighed. Yes, she realized that type of metaphor was for schoolgirls and fairy tales, but ...

"Hey, Honor, come here, please," Sage called from the office. She wiped her hands and headed to the office. She stopped at the doorway. Her computers were in there, and she wasn't allowed to be around them. "What's up?"

Sage held up his phone. "There have been

three calls from Jewell, but I can't get the connection to hold to place the call back to them. Do you know any tricks?"

She leaned against the door jamb. "If I had my computers up and running, I could try to boost the signal using the technology that the iridium base stations use. It increases the power about tenfold, but ..." She lifted her hands. "I can't."

Sage nodded, and the phone rang again. He answered it and put it on speaker, motioning for her to come closer. Honor stepped into the office and moved away from her computers directly to where Sage was standing behind the desk. "Yo."

"Sage ..." There was a screech of static, and both Sage and she moved away from the phone as the sound assaulted their ears. "Bratva," the static overwhelmed the connection again. "Honor's computer."

"What? Repeat?" Sage almost yelled the words at the phone.

"Tracked ... location ... computer." Then the connection ended.

Sage tried to call Jewell back, but there was nothing to connect to. A gust of wind rocked the house, and a deluge of rain pummeled the roof and siding. Honor rubbed her arms. "The Bratva tracked my location from the computer?" She looked at Sage. "To Dallas?"

Sage pulled a laptop out of a drawer and opened it up. "Or here." He messed with the computer. "Damn it." He glanced at her. "If the Bratva tracked you via your computer, how would they do it?"

She glanced over at her laptop. "They would have modified the program I had open, the messenger program. It's always running in the background. If I were them, I'd have the computer ping locations off cell towers so I could watch in real time where I was going."

"Would the computer have to be on?"

"Yes."

"That computer was on all the way here." Sage pointed at her laptop.

She nodded. "Yes. They could track us to the nearest cell tower. Finding us after that would be a process of elimination."

"They've had time to find us, depending on where they were bringing people in from ..." Sage stared at the ground. "But the hurricane could have impeded their progress."

"Do you really think they'd follow me? Why?

They could hire any black hat programmer on the dark web."

Sage sat down and pulled her into his lap. "The program you originally made for them ... Has anyone else made that kind of program?"

Honor sighed and thought for a moment. "No, not that I've seen."

"And in your position, you'd know."

She nodded. It was true. Working with the computer systems and security Jewell kept them fully updated on all the new attempts to defeat security systems. All classified at the highest level, and none she'd seen in the years since she destroyed the Nutcracker had been able to virtually bore through firewalls in the manner of the program she'd authored. "Yeah, I watched. In case they'd maintained a copy of the program, which anyone with half a brain would have done."

Sage nodded. "Alright, we're going to assume the Bratva is coming for you because they want the program you authored or some variance of that program. That's the only logical step that makes any sense."

She nodded. "But I won't make them another program. They can't have it."

Sage turned and looked at her. "Did you maintain a copy of it?"

Honor blinked, for some reason shocked that he'd asked, but she nodded. "I have a copy on my primary computer."

"The box," Sage clarified.

"Yes." She lifted her thumb to her mouth and bit what little nail she had left. "If they took that computer, they'd have access to it."

"Then we hide that computer and ensure you are inaccessible."

"What?" She sat up and rubbed her arms. God, she needed a drink.

"Listen." The wind died down, and the rain had let up.

"Call now?" She grabbed his phone and handed it to him. He dialed quickly. "Sage?" Zane answered the call.

"We won't have long. The feeder bands are moving in and out."

"The Bratva installed a tracker to the messaging program on your secondary computer." Jewell spit the words out so fast it sounded like one long word.

"That's what we figured out from your previous calls," Honor confirmed.

"Why?" Zane spat out.

Sage spoke quickly, "The program Honor developed for them, it's on her primary computer. The only thing that makes sense is they want the program or her to produce the program for them."

"I found it when I was going through the system. I haven't opened it, but I did put a fence around it. Is it dangerous to our systems?" Jewell asked for input from Honor.

Honor answered immediately, "Not any longer. The tweaks I suggested throughout the years have rendered it ineffective against Guardian. Any agency that isn't up to Guardian's standard in computer safety is vulnerable."

"Which is over ninety-five percent of all government and private industry," Jewell added.

"They could be in your area," Zane said just before there was an extended scratch of static.

"I'm on it," Sage said when the static cleared.

"We'll send down help," Zane offered.

"They won't get here in time. Honor is safe in the house with the hurricane shutters closed. It's a fortress. I'll hide her computer and post myself outside."

Honor sprang to her feet. "What? The wind is over a hundred miles an hour!"

"I'll be alright." Sage stood, too. "Zane, what authority am I working under?"

"Archangel has authorized up to Thorn Team Red protocol. Honor and that system are an asset that cannot be compromised. Do you copy?" Zane's voice was hard and sharp as a flint.

Sage lifted his eyes to her, and a small tip of his lips happened before he acknowledged, "I copy up to Thorn Team Red protocol approval."

"I've been running a scan for the car parked outside your Dallas apartment. It's new enough to track via the installed software. I found it in New Orleans, but since the storm came in, I've lost it."

"They wouldn't send the same people." Sage shook his head.

"If they wanted to deal with the losers who let you go, they'd take care of them while they were taking care of you and gaining access to Honor," Zane said before a long string of static sounded.

Sage nodded. "Or the people hunting us aren't on a sanctioned Bratva operation, and they need the manpower." The wind roared into the house again, seeming to shift the building under her feet. It wasn't a surprise when the call dropped.

"You can't go out there." Honor pointed to the

window in the office that was sealed off by the hurricane shutters.

"I can, and I will." Sage moved over to her. "I'm going to gear up. I need to know you'll be okay."

"Okay? Okay? No. No, I'm not okay." A crack of thunder rumbled through the house. "You could be killed out there!"

He put his hands on her shoulders. "Honor, if I don't go out there, we both could be killed. I'm taking the box with me. I know where to hide it."

"Just destroy it! Jewell has a ghost of my hard drive."

Sage cocked his head. "Can you wipe it out?"

"My computer? Yeah, with a handful of keystrokes." She stared at him.

"Good." He walked across the room and grabbed the computer. "Wipe this one. I'm taking this with me."

"That one? That's the one with the messaging app on it. I've had that forever. It isn't my primary. It doesn't have the program on it any longer. Hell, it doesn't even have the same hard drive. I destroyed that after I moved the program to my primary computer."

"But it's the one that Dean would recognize, right?"

She blinked up at him. A small smile pulled at the corner of her lips. "Yes." Then her brow furrowed. "What are you going to do with it?"

"I don't know, but it could be used as bait." Sage winked at her. "When you have a rat, you bait the trap with the food they want the most."

"How do you know Dean will be out there?"

"Because he let you slip through his fingers in DC, and the goons he sent to Dallas couldn't get the job done. His superiors want results, and he's been stalking you for a long time." Sage took the other computers and walked over to the floor-to-ceiling bookshelf. He pulled the middle shelf toward him, opening his way into his safe room, where he stored his weapons and a few essentials. Sage placed his thumb on the keypad and waited for it to unlock. The solid locks clanked as they opened. He pushed the door in and turned on the light.

"Wow," Honor said from beside him. "Are you expecting a war to break out?"

Sage looked at the small armory and shook his head. "No, but I'm ready for one if it comes." He placed her primary computer and the other laptop in an open safe before he closed it and spun the old-time dial.

"Okay, ummm ... I'm going to go wipe the laptop." Sage pulled a tactical holster off the peg and wrapped it around his waist. He also hooked several ammo pouches to his belt. The weapons were well-oiled and could withstand the water onslaught in the short term. He holstered his Mark XIX Desert Eagle fifty caliber handgun. The weapon could take down an elephant or a ghost from Honor's past. With the Thorn Team Red protocol approved, he had permission to take out, by whatever means necessary, the people who were after his asset.

He'd trained enough with Smoke to know more about explosives than most people on the Thorn Teams. He went to the shelf and selected what he'd need. Underwater demolition was his old partner, Smoke's passion. Sage grabbed the equipment that would work underwater or above ground. If the bastards were out there or coming for them, they'd have one hell of a surprise. He placed the explosives, detonation charges, det cord, pins, and a couple of surprises inside a small pack before he grabbed and strapped a 911 Interceptor to the top of his boot. The knife was an oldie but a goodie. He fitted the lightweight body armor over his head and tightened it to fit snuggly. Sage turned off the light but left the door open.

Honor was sitting at the desk, staring at a blue screen on the computer. She turned when he walked out of the saferoom. "I'm leaving the access door to the safe room open. If you need to, you go in there and close the door. It is the safest place in the house."

"I'm scared." She shut the lid on the computer and handed it to him.

Sage pulled her in and held her tightly. "I'm going to take care of everything." He kissed her quickly because he had no idea how much time he had—if any at all—before the Bratva found its way to them. "I've got to go."

14

Sage got into the small chute under his desk, balancing on the ladder's rungs. "Put that flooring back in, just the way I told you." He stared up at Honor.

"We're safe in here. You said so yourself. You don't need to go out there." She dropped to her knees. "Please, Sage."

He moved up one rung and kissed her. She was safe in the house because he'd make sure of it. He had no idea what the bastards would do, and blowing up the house wasn't outside the scope of imagination when dealing with an organization like the Bratva.

"Close the floor up and make sure the panels match. That locks it from the inside. When I want back in, I'll knock four times from whatever door I'm at. Four times."

"You'll be back, right?" Honor's hand shook as she started to reach for his cheek. She pulled back quickly as if burned. Sage reached for her hand and placed it on his cheek. Her fingers and palm were cold, and he could sense her fear. "I want you to touch me, Honor. Never doubt that. I'll be back."

"What if you don't come back? What do I do?"

"The satellite phone is on the desk if you need it. Hand me your computer." He waited for her to hand it to him. "I'll be back." He kissed her again and turned on the flashlight attached to his belt before heading down the ladder. To her credit, the light from the house extinguished. He glanced back up and pointed the flashlight at the floor. As the planks slid back into place, the iron bars slid across the small portal. Even if they opened it, they wouldn't be able to move the bars. That was only possible from the bottom of the shaft.

Sage made his way to the bottom and sat in the small crawl space as he wrapped the computer in clear plastic and wedged it between the ladder and the cement bricks. He'd have it if he needed it for negotiation. He also portioned the explosives, wrapped them, and bundled them together with the detonation pins, wire, and remote detonators. Those bundles were wrapped in plastic and placed in his pockets for quick access. He turned off the flashlight and attached it to his vest before he unlatched the bricks and pushed to open the access panel.

Knowing the bricks were unlocked, he should have been able to open the door, but it wasn't moving. Sage sat down on the wet cement, braced his back against the interior wall, and used his legs to push open the panel. A flood of water came into the small crawl space. *Shit*. He pulled in a lungful of air and held his breath as the water rushed in. Sage kept his legs braced to keep the door open. When the water filled the crawl space, he felt the pressure on his legs relax. Sage leveraged his hands over his head and ejected himself feet first from the crawl space.

Sage grabbed the blocks once he was outside and lifted slowly out of the foul-smelling river water that had been pushed up out of its banks. He kept close to the bricks and wiped his eyes.

The wind battered him, stinging his skin with its force. Sage oriented himself and turned around, peeking over the cement bricks. The sideways slanting rain obscured his vision, but he couldn't miss two vehicles at the end of the drive by his mailbox. The road dipped, and the depression was a river swirling with debris and, more than likely, snakes flooded out of the low-lying marshy area by the river.

Sage didn't move as he scanned the area. The men could still be in the vehicles, or they could have deployed, and he didn't want to become a target if they were surrounding the house. There was higher ground to his left. They'd have to go through the water, but that was where he'd go. Sage carefully shifted so he could see the road leading up the embankment where he'd parked his truck. Bingo. One, no ... three men were hunched down beside his truck. That was the back side of the house. Sage lowered until just his head was out of the water and moved around the brick structure, scanning the front of the house. Ah, there ... three men were on a small knoll holding onto an azalea bush his mom had planted when he was young. Sage couldn't hear them, but there was obviously a discussion going on about how to get to the stairs with the flooding water from the river raging by them. The current was strong, and Sage would use it to float unseen to the embankment.

He pushed off and took a breath, submerging

and letting the current take him. The force of the flow of water pushed him into the earthen berm. Sage slowly lifted his head out of the water and pushed back farther into the dirt bank. He couldn't see the front of the house, but he prayed Honor would listen to him and get into the safe room if she heard anything that sounded like someone trying to get inside the house.

The wind roared, slapping his wet hair across his face. Sage didn't even try to fight it; instead, he turned and let the water push him farther down the bank. He started his climb. The dirt was soaked, and the mud pushed down as he grabbed it and tried to climb. He made small gains and huge losses as the bank crumbled under his weight and the driving rain. It took him too fucking long, but the wind and rain of the latest feeder band were as much a detriment to the men by his truck as they were to him. Sage hauled himself onto the level ground and rested a minute, sucking in huge lungsful of air. He low crawled toward the truck. The three men in front of him were fixated on the house. He could hear their voices as they shouted at each other. The words were completely lost in the onslaught of wind. It didn't matter. *Red protocol.* He wouldn't ask them why they were surrounding his house during a Cat Two hurricane. Sage made it to his truck and shimmied under it. He pulled the Interceptor 911 out of its sheath. The blade was honed to a sharpness that almost defied logic. Sage waited. The wind and rain were less intense under the truck, and he could hear their words now.

"Out in a fucking hurricane, for what? A fucking woman," one of the men yelled into the wind.

"Not a woman, her skills," a second voice yelled over the wind.

"Shut up. You stupid fuckers lost her in Dallas. The boss wants this woman for barter. Watch for the signal. Then we nuke this fucking house."

Sage had heard enough. He slid within inches of the men and drew his weapon. With the 911, he made a wide arch and slashed through the wet jeans and boots, cutting tendons at the men's ankles. The last man he had to hack twice, but the screams and falling bodies told him he'd hit his target.

Slithering out from under the truck, he lifted the first man off his face. Fat boy from Dallas. "Remember me?" Sage yelled at the man before he dragged him to the edge of the embankment and let him tumble into the water below. He turned just as knife dude lifted his revolver. Sage pushed to the left as the gun fired. He spun and hit the truck when the bullet hit his arm. It stung like a bitch. Sage lifted his other arm and fired his Desert Eagle. The thunderous explosion would alert the people on the other side of the house. He glanced down at his arm. Thank God, just a bullet burn. He literally dodged that bullet. Sage grabbed the man left alive and pulled him behind the truck, ducking down to remain as invisible to the people on the other side of the house as possible. "Who are they bartering her to? Tell me, and I may let you live."

"If I tell you, he's going to kill me. I'm dead either way." The man spit the words at Sage.

"Dead either way?" Sage holstered his weapon and grabbed the knife from where he'd dropped it. "Skinned alive dead is a hell of a lot different than shot dead." Sage grabbed the man's ankle, the severed tendon a ball at the back of his leg.

He glanced up to make sure there was no one approaching from the house side of the property and grabbed the man's ankle, inserting the tip of the knife under the skin. He didn't care if he had to strip every piece of epidermis from the man. He'd find out what the Bratva was bartering Honor for.

Sage began to slice, and the man's scream ripped across the whaling wind. "More money! He wants more money for her and the computer shit she does."

Sage dropped the man's ankle. "From who?"

"I don't know. A woman. She wants a programmer who can get into someplace secure."

"How were you going to nuke my house?"

"Grenades to the pilings."

"Where are they?" Sage growled the words.

"The guy you threw down the bank had them."

Sage pulled the man's weapon out of his holster and jacked all but one round out of the magazine. He handed the man the magazine and the automatic. "One bullet. Make it count." Sage lifted in a lunge and jumped down the dirt embankment, rolling into the rising waters at the bottom. The swift current carried him an incredible distance before he managed to grab a branch of a low tree. He pulled himself up and out of the raging waves that were getting stronger. Sage moved as fast as he could. Debris crashed into him, and he leaned into the wind, angling his body toward the ground to move into the stinging torrent. A flying branch caught him across the face, slicing his cheek and sending him to the ground.

Sage pushed back up and worked his way to his house to Honor. As he approached the house, he scanned for the men he knew were alive. He saw one on the front steps. The man wasn't looking toward him but into the water. He pointed and then jumped up two steps, yelling and looking over his shoulder. Sage dropped to his knee and wiped the hair from his eyes. Another man was waist-deep in the water. The third stood on the knoll. That was the man he was going for. Sage backed up and moved down and around. The river had forked back about a quarter mile. He'd be able to cross it quicker and move behind the man on the knoll.

Sage heard several gunshots, carried to his downwind location by the tumult of wind. A vivid strike of lightning hit behind the house. The immediate roar of thunder vibrated the ground under his feet. Sage found the spot he was looking for, backed up, and sprinted toward the water. Well, sprinted was a relative term. His clothes soaked and the ground soft and muddy, he gathered as much speed as he could. He jumped and stretched for the other bank. His grasp slipped, his hands clutching at nothing, sliding and being sucked back into the water through the silt and mud. The current took him a short distance, but he managed to grab ahold of an outcropping of weeds. He elbowed up into the mud and kicked his way free of the current.

Gasping for air, he pushed himself up and moved. If that fucker made it across the river, he and the other could start prying the hurricane shutters open. It would take time, but they'd be able to get into the house.

Sage trudged through the mud. The effort to pull himself through the thick, sucking clay soil would have been impossible to keep up if he hadn't trained so fucking hard at the Annex. Thank God for those maniacs, Dixon and Drake. He dropped to his knees at the sound of another gunshot.

Sage scanned the area. The man on the knoll was shooting at the water. A realization curled his lips into a sneer. The fucker was busy, and that was his chance. He trudged up unnoticed as the man shot again into the water. Sage lifted his Desert Eagle and slammed the fucker down across the man's skull.

Deadweight dropped into the water-soaked

ground at his feet. As Sage lifted his Desert Eagle, both men on the bottom of the steps lifted their hands. Wrong answer. "In the water!"

The men looked at the water and then at each other. Sage pulled the trigger shattering the step beside one of them. Still, they didn't move. Sage was ready for it. They swung as one and fired at him.

Sage stood his ground and fired. He saw the guns buck in the men's hands before he heard the report. The strong buck of the fifty caliber was probably why he missed the second man. It was no surprise that fucker fired again.

A searing pain at his side sent him to his knees. Sage dropped into a prone position, cupped the bottom of his firing hand, and sent three bullets into the man across from him. The guy's body bucked in concussive throws of ragdoll contortions. Sage made sure there was no movement from across the torrent before he moved to check his side. Fuck. He pulled his ammo belt off and lifted his vest. A burrow the size of two fingers along the top of his hip flooded with blood. As far as he could see, there weren't any organs falling out, and he was still in danger with the unconscious fucker beside him.

Sage moved, hissing at the searing pain over his hip. "F-fucker." When he realized he stuttered, Sage screamed at the top of his lungs. He glared at the son of a bitch who was flopped face up in the water. "Should have fallen face down," Sage said into the wind. He grabbed the man's weapons and his wallet.

Sage sat there, bleeding and in pain, needing a way across the flood waters. "What the fuck are you going to do, Browning?" he murmured as the wind drove the rain at him with a force that would have hurt if he weren't already numb to the stinging.

Watching the current as it split at the knoll, Sage blinked. Could he ... He reached into his pocket and pulled out a bundled explosive. He looked at the path of the water around the knoll. *What if ...*

Sage stood and unwrapped the explosive bundle. He shoved the det cord and detonation pin into the explosives before he attached the end of the cord to the device, that small charger that would send the electronic impulse to the detonation pin. He did the same to the other. Sage walked to the far side of the knoll and dropped both bundles into the water. The current started to take them, but Sage sank to the ground, covered his ears, and hit the ignition charge.

The concussion of the explosion lifted him off the ground. Huge globs of mud rained down on him after a heavy wave of river water pushed him toward the house. Sage grabbed at the unconscious man as they both were carried toward the raging current of flooding river water that ran in front of his house.

Only it wasn't a torrent anymore. Sage sat up. It worked. *It actually fucking worked.* He'd diverted the flood waters, at least temporarily. He groaned as he stood and grabbed the unconscious bastard by the collar. He dragged the son of a bitch across the water and onto the bottom step, then stopped there to catch his breath and divest the dead bodies of their weapons. Sage pulled the dead weight up three steps, stopped, sat down, and rested. It was a pattern he followed until he reached the top. He dropped the man to the deck and walked over to the door. With his fist, he pounded on the shutter four times.

He waited and waited. Finally, the latch on the hurricane shutter was released from the inside. The shutter slammed open, catching him in the face. "Fuck!" Sage grabbed the door and looked at Honor, who was holding a rifle on him.

"Sage! Oh, my God!"

"Hold the door," he yelled as he struggled with the door and what he suspected was a broken nose.

Honor grabbed the door and braced herself as she held it open. Sage moved back to pick up his one remaining assailant and dragged him past Honor, dumping him on the floor. He helped Honor shut the door, and they relatched the heavy metal bar.

"Your face is bleeding! There was an explosion! I heard it. And gunfire, sporadic, but it was gunfire. I heard it." Honor almost danced in front of him, wanting to touch him but probably not knowing where she could.

He dropped his hand on her shoulder. "I need big zip ties from the safe room." It took her a second, but she spun, jumped over the man he'd thrown on the floor, and raced through the living room into the office. He looked at the rifle she'd held on him. The M-4 had a magazine loaded. He reached for it and pulled the charging handle back, ejecting a round. Well, fuck him standing. Honor knew a thing or two, didn't she? He looked at her when she ran back into the living room. "You know how to fire an M-4?"

"Yes. Jewell's husband made sure all of us knew how to fire several types of handguns and that kind of rifle. It's a fun day every six months or so, but no one ever thought we'd have to use them. There was an explosion. Did you hear it?" Honor handed him the zip ties.

Sage wiped his wet hands on his wet jeans, doing absolutely nothing to dry his hands. He took the plastic and gripped it tightly in his wet hands. "Yes, I caused it. I had to divert the water to get across to the house."

Honor seemed to dance from one foot to the next, her arms wrapped around herself. "Are we safe?"

"Now. Yes." Sage grabbed the man's hands and zip-tied them behind his back using three separate ties so the bastard couldn't go Navy SEAL and break the damn things. Jesus, his nose ached like a motherfucker. It was broken. Of that, there was no doubt. Sage lifted his prisoner's feet, zipped them together, then linked three ties together, strapping the man's knees together.

"Do you know him?" Sage grabbed some filthy

wet hair and lifted the man's face, tilting it toward Honor.

She nodded. "That's Dean." She wrapped her arms around herself and stepped closer to Sage.

He stood up and hissed, grabbing his side. Man, that wound hurt like a bitch. Sage grimaced. "He's not going anywhere. He can't break the zip ties if he can't gain momentum." Sage ripped the Velcro tab on the side of his vest and cracked the thing open. Yeah, that wasn't looking too good.

"Oh, my God, you've been shot!" Honor gasped.

"More than once." Sage glanced down at his arm. He was lucky on both accounts. "We need to get ahold of Jewell."

"You need to get medical attention first. That water wasn't clean, was it?"

Sage shook his head. "As far from it as it could get."

"Go take a shower. Where's your medical kit?"

"In the safe room."

"Wait here while I get it, then go clean up and put a towel on those wounds after you wash them with soap and water." Honor bolted to the safe room again, jumping over the bastard Benedict. He heard something crash.

"Are you okay?" Sage called out to Honor. The man on the floor groaned. Sage looked down at him. "I wasn't talking to you fuckwad."

"I'm fine. I'm fine! I accidentally dumped some stuff out of a box looking for this." She ran back with a large pack marked with a red cross.

Sage put his hand on her shoulder, tired as fuck and hurting. "Some things in that room don't like to be dropped. They could go boom."

Honor looked back toward the safe room and, with wide eyes, turned back to him. "Sorry? Now, go before you get an infection."

If it was going to be infected, it already had ample opportunity, but he understood where she was coming from. He'd make it quick. Sage handed her the M-4. "Sit over there." Honor did as he said, holding the weapon with the barrel pointed toward Dean. "Take the safety off."

There was a very distinct metal click. The man tied beside him heard it. He stopped his slow movements and held still. Sage nudged the bastard with his boot. "You try to move, and she'll kill you. She has every motive, and she's not the woman you used to know."

Honor smiled up at him and leaned back in the chair. "I won't hesitate."

Sage nodded and headed back to the bathroom to clean up. He wouldn't be gone long, but any time in that fucker's presence was too long for Honor. That bastard would try to fuck with her again.

15

Honor's hand shook as she held the rifle. She prayed Sage hurried. Dean moved, though the zip ties gave him little latitude to adjust his position. He turned his head and opened his eyes. Blinking, he stared at her for several long minutes before laughing.

Honor's hand stopped shaking. The bastard was laughing at her, and she had the upper hand. She moved the barrel of the M-4 until it was pointed at Dean's head. He stopped laughing then.

Dean's voice was flat when he spoke, "So, the fat, ugly programmer turned into a swan and thinks she's big now that she has a gun."

Honor didn't say a word. He didn't deserve her thoughts or her attention. She cocked her head and looked at the man who'd caused her so much misery. It was strange, but he'd seemed so much … well, *more* when they'd been dating. But his narrow-set eyes and crooked smile weren't the mesmerizing material they'd once been—when she'd been desperate for love. When she hadn't known how a true man acted or how a man of integrity treated a woman.

"You've changed."

Honor shifted her gaze and cocked her head the other way. Measuring him against Sage, the man lacked in every category. She once again didn't respond. Instead, she simply stared at him.

Dean spat, "I want that program."

She snorted.

"I can make you rich beyond your wildest dreams. We'll have everything we've ever wanted."

Honor moved the barrel of the weapon up and down a bit. "I have everything I've ever wanted." And that was the truth. She had her tenuous hold on her sobriety, she had a new and exciting relationship with a man she could respect, and if God heard her prayers, she'd have a job with Guardian. If not, she'd find something to do.

"They know about you. They'll keep coming after you."

"Who? The Bratva? I don't think so. Guardian will make sure I'm safe." She shifted in her chair and sighed. "You have no leverage. You're going to jail."

"The Bratva? God, no." Dean struggled with the zip-ties.

She shook her head. Again with the lies. "The men in Dallas were Bratva."

"They're hired meat. Men who used to be connected and are desperate for money. Let me go, and I'll take you to the people who can and will run the world one day. My cousin and uncle were set to take over the right arm of the organization. They needed just a bit more funding. Guardian fucked them over. It's a good thing your precious Guardian is a crumbled heap. They'd be the first target."

Honor saw Sage coming out of the bedroom. He put his finger to his mouth and then rolled his hand, asking her to keep Dean talking.

Honor sighed, "Who are these people? The all-powerful, mighty men behind the emerald curtain with the smoke machines?"

"People only I can introduce to you." Dean licked his lips. "That program is worth you're weight in gold." He was able to tip a bit, so he was almost on his side. "You could name your price."

Honor cocked her head to the other side. "You know, I don't believe a word that comes out of your mouth. You're a liar and a thief. Why should I ever believe you?"

"The money is there. Millions, just waiting for me ... for us. That program could make you very rich." Dean's voice rose to a desperate pitch.

"You mean the money would make *you* rich? You'd steal it from me. No, I don't think so. Not this time."

"It would be different," Dean offered.

"How?" Honor licked her lips. The urge for a drink was as large as an elephant and sitting on her gut with a crushing weight.

"Once they get the program, you'd have your money, and I'd be gone. You could come with me. Another country." Dean seemed to be grasping at straws.

"Why?" She sighed. "Being dumped in a foreign country sounds wonderful. No, you haven't changed. I've learned my lesson. There's nothing you could tell me that would make me want to give you that program."

"There's a revolution coming," Dean hissed.

"Let me go, and I'll take you with me. You loved me once. I bet you still do."

Honor laughed and shook her head. "God, I was so naïve. I never loved you. I was desperate for attention, and you used me and stole from me. Go to hell."

Dean glared at her. "You're a fat, ugly cunt!"

"Ah, there's the Dean I know. Your lowbrow language is unflattering, but your lack of originality is insulting." Honor stood up. "Did you hear?" She looked over from Dean to Sage.

"Almost every word." Sage extended his hand to her, and Honor walked over and laid the M-4 on the kitchen table. Sage folded her into his arm as his other hand held a towel to his side. He dropped a kiss to her lips, and she leaned into him. "After we take care of bandaging me up, we'll call in. The winds are abating." Sage loosened his hold on her. She looked up at him. Her handsome knight in shining armor had been through hell. His nose was swollen, and there were red and purple slashes under his eyes. A cut across his cheek and an angry gash on his bicep. Then there was the bullet wound at his hip.

She lifted her hand and cupped his cheek, whispering, "You went out there for me."

Sage smiled at her. "You're worth so much more than a few bruises. Never forget that. You are worth so much more." He dropped a kiss on her lips.

Honor let the kiss fade and dropped back down to her feet from her toes. "Let me take care of you."

"Gladly." Sage sat down; his dry jeans were unbuttoned. He held a clean towel to his side.

Honor glanced over at Dean, who was glaring at them. The saying, "If looks could kill," well, that applied to Dean at that moment. She turned her back on the man and opened the medical kit. "What happened to your nose?" she asked as she dug for antibiotic cream and bandages.

"When you released the hurricane shutter, it flew back and cracked me. I was able to straighten the bones while I was in the shower. It bled like a river for a hot minute, but I got it to stop."

She froze with bandages halfway out of the pack. "I did that to you?"

Sage shook his head slowly. "No. The door and the hurricane-force winds did this. You didn't do anything wrong." He put his free hand on her hip. "Are we communicating here?"

He stared at her until she smiled and whispered back to him, "Yes, I hear what you're saying." He was so diligent about making her understand his words. He was the epitome of an example of how a man should be with a woman. How had she gotten so lucky?

Dean struggled with the zip ties again. "I can't feel my hands or feet."

"Good," Honor and Sage said at the same time.

Honor tipped back her head and laughed before she sobered and touched his cheek. "I'm sorry about the door, even if I didn't cause it." Honor wiped the cut on his cheek and spread some anti-biotic ointment on it. She did the same for the bullet burn on his bicep, then put a nonstick medical pad over it and wrapped gauze around the covering to hold it in place.

She went to her knees in front of him. "I don't know what to do about this. It got all that nasty water in the wound. I think you'll need to be seen by a doctor."

"We're calling in the cavalry. Right now, we're just going to cover it and wait until things are less crazy. The bleeding has stopped for the most part. Just grab one of those elastic bandages out of the bag and wrap it around my waist to keep the hand towel in place." Sage leaned forward so she could do as he instructed. "Could you get the satellite phone for me?" Sage smiled at her, grabbing her hand before she turned. "And, babe, take your time. I need a minute with our guest."

She glanced back at Dean and then at Sage. "All right."

Honor grabbed the garbage from the bandages and put it in the trash before she hopped over Dean and walked into the office. She picked up the phone and sat down on the chair, listening.

"I have the program," Sage said loud enough for her to hear. Honor gasped and then covered her mouth. "Do you want to make a deal?"

"Let me go."

"Make me an offer I can't refuse," Sage said.

"Where's the program."

"Her computer is wrapped in plastic below us, safe and dry."

Honor blinked. But ... her computer was wiped clean. Oh ... she smiled. Sage was getting information from him. God, her heart had flopped for a moment.

"Ten million."

"Fifteen," Sage shot back.

"Deal."

"Who am I giving this program to?"

"Me," Dean hissed.

"No. I'm in on the deal all the way to the top."

"They won't see you. It's taken me years to gain their trust."

"If you made my cut fifteen million without blinking, you're making a hell of a lot more. I've taken out your men, I can kill you, but I won't because I like money, and I have no loyalty to Guardian. A name and an organization, or you don't get the program. She's shown me how the Nutcracker works. I know what it can do."

Honor tiptoed to the door and peeked around the corner. Dean was facing Sage. "What do you want?"

"As I stated, a name and an organization. I want something, or you get nothing."

"How do I know you'll deliver."

Sage smiled. "You don't, but it's your only chance." Sage lifted off the floor, walked back to the table, and sat down. "I want a house like this. I want enough money to disappear forever. Another country is fine. But why leave? This is America, man. There isn't going to be a fucking revolution."

"You have no idea what's coming. Her name is Xena."

"Why do I want to leave?"

"She's acquired radioactive material to make bombs. Do we have a deal?"

"I told you I needed an organization." Sage went into the kitchen and got a knife from the butcher block. "I'll cut these ties, and we'll get comfortable until the storm passes."

Honor listened to the wind outside. It had stopped, but there was a gentle rain falling on the metal roof of the house.

"I don't know. I don't think she's part of an organized group."

"With millions to throw around to gain access to a program? She has to be connected to something."

"Dude, no one's mentioned a name to me. Do we have a deal?"

Sage snorted and dropped the knife on the counter. "No, you stupid son of a bitch, we don't. Honor, bring me the phone."

Dean let out a string of cuss words. "You can't use any of that information. You didn't read me my rights!"

Sage chuckled. "I'm not a cop. What the fuck do I care about your rights."

"You work for Guardian!" Dean shouted.

"Yeah, but not in that capacity." Sage hit redial on the phone.

"Status."

"Honor and I are secure," Sage immediately said.

"Authenticate Bayou."

Sage rolled his eyes. "Backwoods. I'm going to kill Smoke for that authentication."

"We'll change it, then," Zane replied. "Sitrep."

"One in custody. I have intel and five code reds, four on-premises. I'm going to need medical eventually."

"Define the injuries," Zane said.

"Gunshot to the area above the hip. Not life-threatening, but I was in flood waters, and it needs to be stitched up."

"Is there a place for a bird to land?"

"At the moment, no, but the flood waters will recede quickly. The storm has passed, I believe."

"I need the intel ASAP," Zane grunted. "Local authorities are impossible to reach to take control of this guy, and I need this guy put on ice. Next time I remodel, I'm building a jail cell."

"You can reach them," Honor said from beside Sage, where she'd been listening to the conversation.

Sage handed her the phone. "We can reach them," she said again.

"How?" It was Jewell who asked the question.

"On the sat phone. It should be possible to reach a ham radio operator by connecting to a terrestrial network instead of a satellite network, right?" Honor itched for a computer.

"Oh, my gawd, that is brilliant. Okay, so we can dial the ham radio operators call sign or frequency using the keypad on the sat phone," Jewell added in a rush.

Honor nodded and cut in, "But remember that the ham operator needs to be on the same frequency or network as the sat phone, and we don't know which one the first responders down here are using." She tapped on the tabletop with her fingers. "We'd need to make sure the sat phone is programmed with the correct settings. Frequency, mode, and power to match the ham radio operator's equipment."

"We could build an algorithm that switches each up and down the spectrum. Shit, it'll take forever doing it by myself."

"I could help," Honor hurried her offer. "I know I'm not supposed to …

"You can talk me through it. I'll type. You code.

We need to get this done. Desperate times and all that shit." Jewell spoke so fast it was almost impossible for Honor to understand, but she had years of deciphering Jewell-speak.

"Let me get to the desk." Honor stood and started her way to the office. Dean rolled as she walked past him, and his sudden movement tripped her. Honor fell face forward. The phone went flying, and she tried to put her arms in front of her face to stop the fall. Her head hit the floor, and the hollow thudding noise echoed in her ears. Brilliant lights popped in front of her eyes and exploded around her.

16

Sage exploded across the room and knelt by Honor. She was out cold. He grabbed the phone. "Get a Mercy team here. That fucker Dean just tripped her. She's unconscious, and this is the second or third time in the recent past that she's hit her head and lost consciousness."

"On it."

Sage picked her up, the wound at his side screaming in misery as he stood. He took her to the couch and laid her down. There was a knot forming on her forehead. He stood up slowly and turned around. Dean sneered at him. It was the last mistake that bastard would make.

SAGE PICKED up the phone again and noticed it was still connected. "Sage?" Zane asked. His rasping breath must have given away the fact that he'd picked the phone up.

"Yeah."

"Is the fucker alive?"

Sage looked down at his hand and then over at Dean. That sneer wouldn't have as many teeth the next time the fucker tried to use it. "For now." He glared at the man.

"We've got management coordinating a medical team with the Air National Guard. Most of the units on the Coast have bugged out, but we have one in Texas fueling up and heading your way."

Sage sat down by Honor. "She hasn't woken up yet." He pushed the hair from her face, and rage pulsed through him. "H-he won't l-live to s-see another day." Sage gritted his teeth together.

"She's got a strong pulse, right?" Zane asked.

He touched her neck. The pulse there was strong and steady. "Yeah."

"Then we're hoping for the best. Don't borrow trouble. Give me a brief on what you know."

He knew Zane was trying to keep him calm. He took Honor's hand in his and drew a deep breath. "Six men, two vehicles. Three were positioned behind the house on the embankment, three in front of the house." Then Sage told him exactly what was said. About Honor being bartered and what Dean had said to Honor and him."

Jewell spoke when he finished. "Can you send a picture of this guy? I want to run facial recognition programs on him to find out who the hell he really is."

Sage snorted. "Ain't no one going to recognize his face right now."

"Shit." Jewell sighed.

"I have a driver's license." Sage laid Honor's hand on the couch and went to retrieve the wallet. He may have kicked Dean on the way past. Fucker. He took a picture of it and sent it to Jewell."

"Oh, perfect. Thanks." He heard a keyboard in the background. "Well, that's a fake license. That number doesn't exist," Jewell mumbled. "But the picture is clear, and I'm running it in the system."

"The five Red codes, are they hidden?"

"One was washed away. Two at my front steps and two on the embankment behind the house." Sage stopped. "If the fucker shot himself. If not, he needs medical, too. He has severed Achilles' tendons."

"Ouch," Jewell said in the background.

Sage sat back down beside Honor. Her eyes were moving under her eyelids. "Wake up, baby." He took her hand again.

"Oh, double fucking stuffed bits of dirty data." Jewell's voice drew Sage's eyes from Honor to the phone.

"What?" Zane asked, and Sage listened to a lot of nothing for about thirty seconds.

"Sage, we've got to alert management."

"What?" Honor's hand twitched in his when he spoke.

"Dean is actually Erik Dean Kowalski," Zane said the name as if it meant something to Sage.

"I have no idea what you're talking about."

"Long story, but he's connected to a very bad player who once worked for Guardian. Your helicopter has just taken off. ETA forty minutes."

"That explains the whole G-Guardian f-fucked my family comment." Sage ground his teeth together and tried to calm down. That fucker had hurt Honor on purpose, and his rage level was pegged to the wall.

"Affirmative. Also, we have a fire team coming

with the medical personnel. They'll deploy as a cordon and keep everyone out until we can get our people down there to do the bag and tag on the rest. Since the Governor of Louisiana has declared a state of emergency, we can use the Army National Guard for a brief time to provide safety and security. Both of which you need. You travel with your prisoner and Honor back to Texas. We'll have Dom Ops pick him up when you land. You stay with Honor."

"I wasn't going to leave her."

"I know," Zane agreed. "Don't kill Kowalski. I'll call with updates if we have any before the airlift gets there."

Honor moaned and shifted. "If he caused any permanent damage, he's m-mine." Sage cleared the connection and watched as Honor started to wake. When her eyes fluttered open, he stared at her pupils. Thank God they weren't fucked up. "Hey," he said, carefully moving her hair from the side of her face.

"What ... Oh, my head." She lifted her hand and hissed when she touched the knot on her forehead.

"Dean tripped you. You hit your head pretty hard." Sage kissed the back of her hand, sitting as he was on the floor beside her. She didn't have to move to see him.

She closed her eyes again. "I was going to help Jewell."

"They found a workaround. The military is flying in to pick us up and take us back to Texas," Sage spoke softly and stroked the back of her hand with his thumb.

Honor licked her lips and opened one eye a slit. "Are you still positive there's no alcohol in the house? It's been a shit kind of day. Well, except for this morning."

Sage chuckled. "I'm positive, and I'll make it up to you."

Honor swallowed hard. "Not your fault."

"I know. It isn't yours either." Sage lifted her hand, and she opened her eyes. "What happened to your hand?"

He glanced at the back of his knuckle. "I may or may not have explained in no uncertain terms that I was unhappy with your ex. Although I can neither confirm nor deny that p-possibility."

Honor reached up and touched his cheek. "I'm okay. I've got a headache, but I'm okay."

Sage nodded. "Still mad."

Honor squeezed his hand. "You can be mad. Jeremiah told me that."

Sage chuckled. "He told me that, too. Although I think he'd draw the line at beating the shit out of a tied-up asshole."

Honor lifted her hand and waved it a bit. "What Jeremiah doesn't know won't hurt him."

"How are you feeling?" Sage asked after a moment of silence.

"Headache." She turned her head right and left and then winced when she tipped it backward. "Stiff neck."

"Are you nauseous? How's your vision?" The more she talked, the more hopeful he was that it was just a concussion, but it was time to see a doctor just to make sure there wasn't any serious damage.

"What do you think will happen? With Guardian?" Honor asked in a quiet voice.

Sage sighed. "You know you messed up by not reporting the breach." He shrugged. "I have to put faith in the people who run this organization. I've never seen or heard of them being unfair to their employees."

"Even those who screw up?"

Sage nodded. "I think the moment this organization forgets that their employees are human and fallible is the day it goes under. No one is perfect." He shrugged again. "But if the worst comes to pass, I'll be at your side, as your friend, and as more."

"You don't need the trouble."

Sage chuckled. "I seem to find trouble no matter where I am. I'm not worried about that." They sat quietly.

Dean groaned. "I gotta piss."

Sage bent backward so he could see the asshole. "You piss on my floor, and you'll get more of the same."

Honor moved to sit up, and Sage hastened to help her. She leaned back on the couch and slid into his side when he sat beside her. "Is the hurricane gone?"

Sage nodded. "We'll get a few feeder bands, but the storm has moved on."

"I want to see the hole." Honor chuckled.

Sage's gut dropped. That didn't make sense. "The hole?"

"Yeah, that the explosion caused. That was a big boom."

"Worse than the thunder?" Sage tried to hide his smile.

Honor groaned. "Do not make me roll my eyes. I think my brain is bruised."

Sage kissed the crown of her head. "I think you may be right. Close your eyes. I've got you."

Honor drew a deep breath and relaxed into him. "Sage?"

"Hmmm?" He answered.

"I might like you more than a lot."

He smiled against her hair. "Right back at you, sweetheart. Right back at you."

17

S age wiped his hands on his jeans and took a deep breath before opening the rehab facility door. He'd dropped Honor off three months ago. The bed became available when Honor was still in the hospital undergoing tests.

She was allowed a phone, so he bought her one and put her on his plan the same day she went into rehab. They texted daily and talked after she reached a certain stage in her stay at the center, and the doctors said she could use her phone. Still, he hadn't seen or touched her since he dropped her off. The idea that she might not feel the same way about him as she did when she walked in those doors was something he didn't want to think about. She hadn't said anything that would lead him to believe that, but damn it, that sliver of possibility had festered until it was a massive sore that he needed to lance. The meeting today would be that lance. He stopped at the desk. "Hi, I'm here to pick up Honor Buchanan."

The person behind the desk thanked him and told him to have a seat as she picked up the phone. He heard the woman say Honor's name as he sat down. The woman stood up. "Sir, she's with the doctor. She'll be out when they're finished."

Sage nodded and glanced at his watch. He was about twenty minutes early. He'd driven down from South Dakota over the weekend. The flurry of meetings after the hurricane had also been the beginning of arranging his future at Guardian. The idea that Joseph had come up with had been daunting at first, but he was ready to assume his role. The only thing in question was Honor's future. The brass was close-lipped on that point. Nothing was leaked. Jewell was beside herself because her brother refused to let her know what the executive decision was regarding her failure to disclose the security breach. Though Sage had talked to Zane and Jewell too many times to count, he still didn't know what the brass had decided. But they would soon.

One of the many closed doors opened, and Sage popped to his feet. He smiled when he saw her. She'd cut her hair and gained some weight, but she looked good. Healthy, and damn, look at that smile.

Honor dropped her suitcase and ran to him. He grabbed her and swung her around. She pulled him down into a kiss, and damn if he didn't hold her up until she broke away to breathe. "I missed you." She kissed him again.

"I missed you more." He put her on her feet. "Are you ready?"

She looked back at the desk. "I am. I signed all the paperwork, and I had my out brief with Dr. Orlando."

"Let's get your case and get gone, then." Sage grabbed her hand and walked back for the case. He picked it up and elbowed out the glass doors he'd entered earlier. "Your hair is cute that way." It was shorter and curly, barely touching her shoulders.

"They brought stylists in, and I was able to ask how to take care of my hair. Man, let me tell you, whatever you want to learn to better yourself, the staff will bend over backward to get you the information."

As Sage opened the door to his new truck, Honor whistled. "Wow, look at this one. What happened to the other one?"

He helped her into the cab and shut the door, then trotted around the other side and got into the cab. "Beau's mom and dad lost both their car and their truck in the flooding. I gave his dad my truck and bought a new one up in South Dakota."

Honor put on her seatbelt and twisted around to look at him. He grabbed her hand and started the truck after he belted himself in. She smiled. "How did that go? The meetings in South Dakota?"

Sage nodded. "Good. I have no idea why they think I'd be the one to select for the position, but it means I can stay at the house and commute when needed."

"So, what's the official title?"

"Independent Operative Supervisor," Sage spit out the mouthful of words. "Which means I'm herding the cats and dogs that don't have any formal chain of command." He still didn't know how many he'd be supervising. But he'd be responsible for running any operations his contractors were involved in and bringing in resources from Guardian as necessary. One thing he established up front was that *he* was a resource that could be deployed to help at his discretion. He wasn't a behind-the-desk kind of guy.

"You'll be perfect for the job." She squeezed his hand. "Where are we going?"

"Well, tonight we have a suite at the W. Tomorrow, we're flying to meet with Guardian's executive council."

Honor's head jerked in his direction. "They've called for me?"

"Yeah. I was told they waited until you were cleared to be discharged to schedule the meeting, but they've reached a decision." And that was all he knew. Chief didn't have any further information when they talked last night.

Honor nodded and drew a breath lifting her shoulders and straightening her back. "Good. I need to get this past me, no matter what the outcome."

"True, but we aren't going to think about that tonight."

Honor smiled at him. "We aren't?"

He shook his head. "No."

"What are we going to do, then?" She blinked her eyes, wide and innocent.

Sage laughed. "I'm sure we can think of a few

things to do to occupy the evening." He lifted his eyebrows a couple of times.

Honor threw back her head and laughed. It was amazing to see her so healthy and her personality open wide.

"Hey, Sage?"

He glanced over at her. "Yeah?"

"Drive faster."

He made it to the hotel in record time.

HONOR HELD Sage's hand in the elevator, and the walk to the hotel room door was the longest she could remember. When he opened the door, she gasped at the city view from the floor-to-ceiling windows. "Wow! How high are we?" She spun and walked backward toward the windows.

Sage shut the door and dropped her suitcase. "I don't remember." He shook his head and stalked toward her.

"You don't want to look at the view, do you?" She laughed and kept backing up. Sage shook his head, still moving toward her. "What do you want, Sage?"

"You," he said as he folded his arms around

her. Honor threw her arms around his neck, and Sage lifted her off her feet. She wrapped her legs around his waist and knew they were walking somewhere, but she couldn't care less where they were going. Being in his arms was exactly where she wanted to be.

The taste of Sage was just as she remembered. The way he held her like she was valuable and precious warmed her soul. After three months of intense counseling, she had a good handle on her issues and knew for a fact Sage wasn't one of them. She held on as they descended onto a soft surface. He lifted away, and she looked around. A huge bedroom and a king-sized bed. Honor pulled off her t-shirt, gazing at Sage as he did the same. Damn, he was amazingly built. Strong with muscles that had muscles. She slid off the bed and took off her jeans, panties, and bra.

A wave of shyness prickled across her, and she dropped her eyes. Sage was beside her moments later, lifting her chin with his finger. "You are beautiful."

"I gained some weight back." She'd learned not to eat to soothe herself. She had an addictive personality, and her doctor believed she used food for comfort, which was so true. Plus, she'd exercised every day. She had no idea exercise could be so rewarding.

"You are beautiful." Sage stared into her eyes, not looking at her nakedness but at her. "Never doubt that. To me, you're the most beautiful woman in the world." He leaned down to kiss her. The heat of his desire pushed up against and branded her stomach as he pulled her in and up.

Somehow, they managed to get horizontal on the bed, and Honor let her hands travel over Sage's shoulders and arms. He'd told her so many times that he wanted her touches when she was in rehab that she'd talked to her doctor about her fear of touching him. She had so much work left to do on herself. But those thoughts didn't have a place there between them. She threaded her hands through his hair and opened her legs, and he settled between them as they kissed and touched, reacquainting themselves. The two times they were together were the best memories Honor had. She held them in reverence. They were her happy place when the work at the rehab became hard. His calls and texts were a link to him that had strengthened her when she wanted to give up. He couldn't do the work for her, but he was there when she was tired, when she was grumpy, and when she was sad. Sage had been solid and present. She'd fallen in love with him a bit more every day. Not that she'd tell him. Not yet.

Sage moved and reached toward the night-stand. "No. I've taken care of birth control." She could feel herself blushing. "I'm on the pill. For almost three months. We're good."

Sage came back to her and dropped a kiss on her lips. "We're better than good." He settled between her legs again, and she felt the tip of his cock at her core. She ached for him. She lifted her hips, and he slid inside of her. The months of want evaporated with the gentle strokes that carefully opened her up. She arched under him, and his mouth found her breast. She gasped and held his head. Not directing him. No, just making sure she didn't shatter into a billion pieces and float away. The touch grounded her to him. Brought her focus to the sensations and the adoration he laid upon her. Sage consumed her in totality, and she'd gladly let him. She trailed her toes up the back of his legs and let her hands move down his back … farther. She gripped his ass as he stroked forward and pushed with her legs bringing him fully into her. Sage stopped and dropped his head to her shoulder. "Babe, I'm not going to last."

"Then make us fly." She kissed his shoulder, and he reared up onto his knees. Sage used her thighs and pulled her closer to him. His thumb found the apex of her sex, and he rolled the little bud, stroking one side and then the other. Honor arched off the bed, pushing into the sensation of Sage filling her and stroking her clit. She fisted the pillow under her head and half gasped, half screamed when she shattered.

Her sex contracted, and the rhythmic flutters were so wonderful that she tightened her thighs and squeezed as Sage stroked inside her. The shattering happened again, smaller that time, but oh, so delightful. She contracted again, tightening around Sage. He threw back his head, and the sound he made sunk into her soul. She'd made him feel that way. He dropped to his arms over her, his elbows locked. Then he opened his eyes and stared at her. "I've missed you."

Lifting her hand, she pushed his long brown hair over his ear. "I was afraid at first that what we had wasn't enough for you."

He dropped down and pulled her with him to her side. "Can I tell you a secret?"

She nodded, staring at him as he shared, "I was worried what we had wasn't enough for you."

She popped up on her elbow. "We're a matched set, aren't we?"

He leaned forward and kissed her. "Perfectly matched."

"I guess we better stick together, then." She looked down, not wanting to see his reaction. His finger once again chucked her chin up, and she drew a shaky breath and lifted her eyes. "I think that is a perfect idea." He pulled her into him and started a series of long, smoldering kisses. Honor rolled onto her back and welcomed him back to the place only he could be. Inside her body and her heart.

They made love. It was slow, passionate, all-consuming, and perfect. Honor lay in his arms again, and they watched the sunset over the city. The bedroom windows faced west, and the golden hue of the setting sun filled the room. "Thank you for this. For this beautiful room and for everything you've done for the last three months."

Sage's fingers played with her hair. "You're worth so much more than this."

She turned and moved to lie on his chest and stare at him. "Tomorrow will be the start of a new chapter in my life."

He nodded. "It may not be easy."

She smiled at him. "Life *is* hard. The relationships we build, nurture, and cherish are what keep us going."

Sage stared at her for a long moment. "Then let's keep each other going."

She saw the emotion in his eyes. The emotion that she shared, and they both knew it was too soon to put into words. "I promise."

He rolled her and stared down at her. "I promise." He dropped for a kiss, and she felt tears gather behind her lashes. Her life, no matter the outcome tomorrow, was filled to overflowing because of the man in her arms.

18

Honor squeezed his hand, and he dropped his arm around her shoulders. They'd flown from Dallas to Denver and were met at the airport and driven into the Rocky Mountains. Their driver was behind a blacked-out window, so there was no information from him about where they were going. Sage couldn't have begun to find his way out of the maze of twists and turns. When they stopped, the doors unlocked, and Sage opened the door stepping out and gazing at what he thought was supposed to be the new headquarters of Guardian Security. He knew the facility was being built, and he'd assumed in Colorado since he'd been told to fly to Denver. Only that didn't compute. The complex was one story and stretched for acres. It wasn't an office structure. It was a ... food processing and warehousing facility. Operational by the looks of the vehicles, trucks, and vans that were backed to the loading docks.

"Wow," Honor said when he helped her out. Sage looked at the parking lot, which was filled with pickups and SUVs. The only person he saw was their driver, standing by his open door.

"The receptionist will assist you. I'll take your bags to your hotel," their driver said.

"What hotel?"

"I'll be back for you, sir." The man shut the passenger door and got into the four-wheel drive Suburban, leaving them in the middle of the parking lot.

"Well, I sure hope so. I have no idea where we are." Honor spun around.

"This is awkward," Sage said, putting his hand on her back and guiding her to the entrance.

"It's a food plant? Or something?" She looked up at him, and he shrugged. He wasn't sure why they were being treated like outsiders. Check that. Why Honor was being treated like an outsider? He still had his clearance, and he'd assumed greater responsibility in the organization. Fuck, he hoped for the best in Honor's situation and had stead-fastly refused to think the worst could happen. But maybe it had. They went in the main double doors.

"Hello. Welcome to Guaranteed Food Solu-tions. Can I help you?"

"We have an appointment, but I'm not sure we're in the right place," Sage spoke for them.

"Ah, yes. Mr. Browning and Ms. Buchanan? If you would, please." The receptionist pointed to their right. As they approached, Sage heard the locks deactivate. The doors opened automatically, and they walked into a small waiting area. The doors shut behind them, and the locks slid back into place.

"Authenticate Bayou." A disembodied voice floated to them from hidden speakers. He recog-nized it anyway. Smoke.

"Backwoods," Sage authenticated before looking at Honor. "I'm going to kill him for that authentication."

Honor chuckled nervously. "You've said some-thing like that before."

The wall behind them slid back, and an elevator door opened. Sage glanced up at the camera and shook his head. "Let's go."

He held her hand, and they entered the car.

The door moved back to secure them inside. He felt the slightest of shudders as the elevator moved, down, he assumed, because there wasn't an "up" that he'd seen. He turned to her, and she looked up at him. "I'll be here for you. Whatever they decide, I'll be here. I promised, remember?"

She nodded her head. Her eyes were wide, and she was pale. "I can do this."

"I know you can."

The door opened several long moments later, revealing Smoke on the other side. Sage sighed. "Dude, I hate you and that authentication."

Smoke grabbed him and pulled him into a hug. "You fucking duck out on me, don't call but once a fucking year, and then almost get killed in a hurricane. I hate you more."

Sage hugged his friend tightly. "You're an asshole, and I call you once a week. Stop overreacting."

Smoke let him go and slugged him on the arm. "That's for not calling when you made it out safely."

"It was a Category Two! We were never in any danger." Well, not from the storm. He reached back and grabbed Honor's hand.

Smoke didn't miss a beat. "Hey, nice to meet

you. You've got people waiting for you. *You* are coming with me." He pointed at Sage and turned around to walk down the hall. "We can catch up."

"No. I'm going where Honor's going." Sage was as blunt as he could be without being rude. Okay, fuck it. He was rude.

"Ah, that's a big negative, my friend. She's meeting with the executive committee, and you weren't invited." Smoke kept walking.

"I'll be okay," she leaned over and whispered to him as they followed Smoke down a corridor. Honor's voice was small, and he fucking hated that he couldn't be there for her.

"She'll be fine. The last time I checked, the executive council was well-fed. They won't eat her alive. Come on. My office is just past where we're dropping Honor off." Smoke lifted his hands, and Sage looked up. The ceilings were braced with interwoven metal. They were inside the fucking mountain. "We went sideways in the elevator."

"Yes, down and sideways. Until you earn the secret decoder ring, you get to ride the shuttle." Smoke slapped him on the back. "A nuke could hit this place, and we wouldn't feel it."

"Good to know," Honor said. She wasn't looking around, and her hand squeezed his tightly.

"All right, Honor, this is you." Smoke said as he stopped and pointed to a set of massive, closed doors.

Sage turned her and dropped a kiss on her lips. "You've got this. I'll be waiting for you."

"All right." She nodded and pivoted back to the doors. "I've got this."

Sage watched her as she went to the door and knocked. The huge brown doors swung in. Sage couldn't see much. *Fuck*. He wanted to be in that room with her.

The door shut behind her, and Smoke dropped the happy-go-lucky routine. "I don't know how long this will take. My office is right there. We can see when she comes out."

"What are they going to do?" He turned to look at his friend.

"If I knew, I would have told you. Which is why they didn't tell me. Come on. We'll sit down and stare at the door together."

Sage grunted and followed Smoke. What he wouldn't give to be a fly on the wall, but obviously, that wouldn't be the case. He sat down and looked at Smoke's office. Gazing around and out into the hall, he turned back and asked, "This couldn't have been built since the Siege."

"Nah, this was a Cold War project built by the United States government and then shuttered in the eighties when the Soviet Union fell. Justin King found the food processing plant, which is fully functional. Someone much higher on the food chain than me found this place. The tunnel through the mountain from that facility was made quicker than I thought it could be. But money talks."

"The receptionist?"

"One of our finest, or she was until she fractured a couple of vertebrae in her back. They operated, and she's mobile. The woman can shoot a gnat off a flea's ass, but we don't want anything to complicate her injury. She actually works as a receptionist for the company. She's paid by both us and the food processing plant. They don't know she's ours. That doorway you entered through is a rented office that we modified. All legit and untraceable to Guardian. Again, they have no access, and only a few people come here through that access point."

"Won't management get suspicious?"

Smoke smiled a big goofy smile. "Nope. We know the person who owns the brand. He's got it covered."

Sage nodded and crossed his legs. "We came in that way because she's getting fired, right?"

Smoke shook his head. "Dude, I really don't know. I'd tell you if I did." They were quiet for a moment. "Is she the one?"

Sage sighed and glanced at Smoke. "It's early still, but ... I think so."

"She feels the same way?"

Sage nodded. "Yeah."

"Well, then, I really hope this works out." Smoke dropped back in his seat. "I'd offer to give you a tour, but I know you won't leave this spot."

"You're right about that." Sage leaned forward and dropped his elbows to his knees.

They were silent a couple of minutes before Smoke leaned back in his chair. "I still love you, man. I'm here for you whatever happens to her."

Sage chuckled. "Dude, you're more than a friend to me. You know that, and I fucking love you, too. That still doesn't make me gay."

They both laughed at the running joke between them. Quiet fell over them before Sage admitted, "You were the only one who saw me back then."

Smoke nodded. "I'd been where you were. People thought you were done, beyond repair.

You weren't. You just needed someone to help you."

Sage turned to look at his friend. "I was going to swallow a bullet. My life was in the toilet. If it weren't for that mission to Cuba, I wouldn't be here."

"Yeah, I know. That's why I latched on and didn't let go. My learning disability mirrored what you were going through with your stuttering. I had no idea about Gus and the shit you grew up with at first, though. I just knew your pain."

"That's all done. Mom is free, and Gus is living out his last days staring out a window at a nursing home. He doesn't remember anything or anyone." Or at least that was what he assumed. He didn't know what a person with advanced Alzheimer's went through when they were lost in their own mind.

"I heard you're taking over the independent contractors." Thankfully, Smoke changed the subject.

"Yeah, Bear, Creed, and a handful of cats and dogs. I just assumed that mission was a one-time patchwork job."

"Nope. From what I understand, the Indies are used to augment when specialties are needed."

"Bear can kick some serious ass." Sage nodded. "Creed is skilled, too, man."

"Have you kept in contact with them? I get texts from Creed. Mostly about boats. Mine is docked down in Key West with him." Smoke asked.

"It's going to kill you being on dry land, isn't it?"

"Nah, I get to help Lycos take care of the baby classes as they come up. Charlie will be here on the daily. Me, I'm on the move and traveling."

"Sounds like the best of both worlds for both of you. Where is Charlie? He glanced out the door. "Is her office near here?"

Smoke laughed again. "Yeah, next to Jason's. She's at the Rose right now. Her quarterly visit to annoy the hell out of Fury."

Sage lifted an eyebrow. "Isn't that rather dangerous?"

"The jokes on her. I just saw him in the hallway about an hour ago. She's going to be mad that she can't poke the bear. But he treats her like one of his kids, and she loves antagonizing him. Plus, she'll run the course five or six times and put a thousand rounds down range to keep her proficiency up. Have you been back lately?"

Sage shook his head. "To the Rose? No. I've

been training with Double D up at the Annex. Not much sense going through the courses until I figure out my role as supervisor."

"I wonder what Bear is up to?" Smoke chuckled. "That man was hell on wheels."

"He's doing good. We text pretty often. He has another black belt in some discipline with a weird name I can't remember. His brother graduated from college and medical school. He's in residency to become a neurosurgeon." Sage chuckled. "Bear said his brother wants to examine his head after he dies to see what makes him tick."

"Sounds like something a brother would say. How are yours, by the way?"

"They're doing okay. Seth, Kevin, and Carter are long gone from Bienvenu and better for it. I'm going to make that place my duty station. I'm comfortable there, and I have roots."

"And assholes," Smoke grumped.

"I haven't heard from either Bergeron or Broussard since the night I went back." Then again, Sage hadn't gone to the bar again, either. He didn't drink much, to begin with, and after dealing with Gus, he'd stopped drinking altogether.

"Yeah, you told me you'd announced that you were home."

"And it felt amazing." Sage chuckled. "It's a good place to stage out of. I can be at Louis Armstrong Airport in an hour if I need to fly out to assist the Indies." He liked that word.

Smoke thumped the desk with a fist. "I'm all about decentralizing the management of the organization."

"And yet here you sit." Sage chuckled. "Centralized as fuck."

"What?" Smoke blustered. "Nope. This complex is off the grid. No one is going to find this place."

"Power and communications can be traced."

"Power is covered by a single panel about five feet wide and five feet long. It generates so much that we have backup batteries filled to max capacity. Comm is a bit more intricate. We decentralized the work locations of CCS. Within the next three years, we'll have communication nodes throughout the world, and all will have off-system power and shielded communications. All data processed by those nodes flow to five independent servers located here in the mountain."

Sage took in the information. And damn it, the Siege was a vicious attack that took out too many good people. Hopefully, those who perished somehow knew about the good that had come from it, the reorganization and the upgraded security features. Guardian would never be wholly vulnerable again. It was time for them to return to the offensive and be the sharpened tip of the war against monsters who preyed on the good people of the world. He glanced at the door where Honor had entered. He prayed she would be part of the legacy, too.

19

Honor walked through the doors and turned to her left. A massive room opened in front of her. The warm colors of mahogany, rich reds, saturated gold, and deep blues made the room feel more like a throne room than an inquisition area. Yet, that was what she was facing. A table ran lengthwise across the room. Behind it, she recognized Jason King, an older man she'd never seen before, then Joseph King, Jacob King, and Jared King. Jewell was nowhere to be seen. Great, no friendly faces. She clenched her hands together into fists and straightened her shoulders.

Jason King stood up slowly, as did the other men. "Honor, thank you for coming. Please have a seat." Jason nodded to the one chair across from them.

She sat down and waited. Saying anything now would be superfluous. "Honor, I would like you to tell me in your words what happened, in as much detail as you can, the night that the security breach occurred." Jason leaned back and took off his glasses staring at her.

Honor croaked something, cleared her throat, and tried again. "I was working the night shift. Jewell was there because, before Zane, Jewell was always there." She didn't drop her eyes but spoke directly to Jason. She wanted him to know the truth, and she was relieved to be telling the absolute truth to those who needed to hear it. "I knew that Dean had taken my program. I worked every spare hour I had to devise and build a program that would not only take out the Nutcracker, as I called it, but take out the entity that was using it. Every night, I scoured the new reports looking for it. I knew they'd use the program; it was only a matter of time."

"Were you aware they would target Guardian?" the older man asked.

"No, sir." She shook her head. "I thought Dean would target a financial institution. All he talked about was money. Having the money to do this or that. I thought he'd steal from accounts, but he'd have to figure out a way to transfer the funds without being traced. The Nutcracker will get you into a system, and you can see what is there. Any action beyond that wasn't in the program." Honor stopped and licked her lips. "That night, I was working with Jewell. She and the other programmers were running like crazy with the previous Archangel's wife's accident, the aircraft, and the explosion at your fiancée, or rather your wife's trailer. Jewell asked me to secure our systems because it seemed like a coordinated attack. As I did, I saw the intrusion point because I knew what to look for in the code. I saw whoever was monitoring the unsecured comms moving toward information that could jeopardize so much more."

Honor took a deep breath and finished, "I ejected the program from the system, and I sent my other program after the source. If it did its job, the source's systems and anything it was connected to was wiped out." She finally lowered her eyes and looked at her nicely painted fingernails. So different from the filthy, cracked, and broken nails that she still saw in her mind's eye. "I covered the breach and didn't report it."

"Why?" That came from Joseph King.

She looked over at him. "Because I didn't want to lose my job. Dean said he'd tell everyone I made the program and gave it to him. I did build it. Anyone who knows my work would know by how I wrote the code. I didn't give it to him, sir. He stole it from me. I was scared, and I was stupid. I wanted to tell Jewell, but the longer I waited ... then when Jewell didn't find the breach, I thought maybe I would be okay."

"That you'd gotten away with the crime," Jared King said.

"Yes, sir. That's correct because I knew it was a crime. I worked so hard to make sure I made up for the breach. I lived and breathed Guardian. It was my whole world. Then, the day before the Siege, Dean literally bumped into me on my way out of the coffee shop, Single Perk, across the street from Guardian Headquarters. He was shocked to see me, and God, I was terrified to see him."

"Why?" Jacob King interjected.

"Because he'd started trying to contact me about seven, maybe eight months before using a chat program that we used when we were together."

"Why did you keep the program on your computer?" the older man asked.

Honor sighed and swallowed hard. "I probably couldn't have answered that before I went into rehab, but working with the doctors there, I now believe I kept the messaging program as a way of punishing myself for what I did. Covering up the breach. Every time I looked at the program, it would remind me of what had happened. I would, if you will excuse the expression, pick the scab to make myself bleed."

"And the alcohol?" Jason asked.

Honor nodded. "When I ran into Dean, he grabbed my arm, and he shook me. He was so mad that I hadn't answered him on the message chat. He could see that I'd read his messages. I'd moved since Guardian, and he couldn't find me. When Dean ran into me the day before the headquarters building blew up, he tried to force me to go with him. He said if I didn't build a program for him, he'd make me and everyone at Guardian pay. I didn't know what he meant, but I used one of the rooms with the cots in it that night because I was too afraid to go home. That he'd be waiting for me outside the building. So, I was there, at work at five … I couldn't sleep, so I went to my workstation early. Only a few of us made it out." A tear trickled down her cheek, but she didn't try to wipe it away. "I took as much money as I could out of the bank, got on a bus, and ended up in Dallas. I rented an apartment, cash. I had my computers, and Dean kept messaging me. He said he hoped I was dead and ... so much more. I bought a bottle of vodka one day." She looked up. "At first, I could control it, the drinking. Then I didn't want to. I wanted to hide, to make it all go away. I thought that Dean had blown up Guardian, and it was my fault."

"You didn't watch the news or read about it on the internet?" Jared asked. Honor could tell by his tone that he didn't believe her.

"I did for the first three or four days. But there was nothing in the news other than body counts. I thought Jewell had died until she reached out to me." Honor sniffed and wiped at her face. "It wasn't my fault."

Jason leaned forward. "No, the Siege wasn't your fault. That is absolutely true."

She nodded. "But the unreported security breach was."

He nodded. "It was. I have a question, and I want an honest answer from you."

Honor stared at him. "Only the truth has

passed through my lips in this room. I will never lie again. Mentally, I wouldn't be able to cope if I told a lie."

Jason steepled his fingers together and looked at her over them. "Do you still want a drink?"

Honor blinked. "Yes." She blurted the word out. "I do. I think, in some way, I always will. But today, this minute, under this stress and this pressure, I choose not to drink. I will always fight that desire, sir. I know that, and I understand it. I have to choose to handle my stresses and pressures, either by going to meetings or talking to my sponsor or doctor, but no one can be responsible for my sobriety except me."

Jason nodded and leaned back into his chair. "We've had a chance to question 'Dean'." He made a finger quote around Dean's name.

"I'm sorry. What does that mean?" Honor mimicked his movements.

Jason nodded to Jacob, who flipped open a folder in front of him. "His real name is Erik Dean Kowalski. Does that name ring any bells?"

Honor frowned and thought. "Kowalski ... isn't that the name of the guy who belonged to Guardian? The one who betrayed us?"

"It is," Jared answered. "Erik Dean is Darren

Kowalski's cousin. It seems the family was working together to gather intel on Guardian."

"But I hadn't been hired when I met Dean."

"But you'd applied." Jacob held up a piece of paper. "You posted on social media that you had applied and hoped your dreams would come true."

Honor blinked. "I deleted all social media when I was hired."

"As is required, but this was the breadcrumb that led Kowalski to you. His job was to get someone to build a program that could breach any firewall. Darren Kowalski got a kick out of the information we gave him about his cousin. When we interviewed him last month, he told us Dean was a dirtbag, and no one thought he'd be able to convince anyone to develop a program. They gave him a million euros to get it produced. Payable only when the program was delivered."

"He got it for nothing." Honor hung her head.

"We've downloaded all the information from your messaging program. We understand what was happening." Jacob cleared his throat and continued, "And from what Darren told us, Erik disappeared with the million euros after dropping the program in the lap of one of their computer techs. The Bratva doesn't want anything to do with

Erik. The men who Sage killed were loosely tied to the Bratva. He probably hired them because he knew where to look for men who would do that type of work for money. Darren Kowalski claimed he never heard from him again."

She glanced up at the men, completely morti-fied because they knew how Dean ... or Erik had gotten the program. "Then why did he try to contact me again?"

"*That* we're still working on." Jacob shut the cover on the file. "But we have also ascertained that Erik never disclosed your location. Bienvenu wasn't compromised for Sage."

"Which leads us to the reason for this meet-ing." Jason leaned forward again. "Honor, we've had time to sift through all the information provided by Jewell. We've examined the facts and talked with Jewell about the system, what you did, and how you did it. You've just explained your reason for making the decisions you made. Addi-tionally, there's more afoot here, which does not involve you, nor should it. We've reached a unani-mous decision about your future here at Guardian."

Honor waited. Her breath caught in her chest. That was it. Dear God, after all that time, that was their judgment. She clasped her hands together tightly to stop them from shaking. A cold chill fell over her like a shower. She waited, each second seeming to last an hour.

Jason picked up the single piece of paper in front of him and continued, "Based on the preponderance of the evidence, we've reached a decision on the matter of your breach of contract, breach of established security protocols, and the breach of our trust."

Honor swallowed hard. Her heart was pounding so loud she had to concentrate on hearing what he was saying.

Jason lifted the paper and read, "Honor Buchanan, you are hereby reprimanded, in writing, for your part in covering up the security breach. You will be demoted from your current position as supervisor and moved to a position within a sub-node that will be directly supervised by Jewell King. Your systems will be forensically checked at random without your prior consent. Your activities will be constrained to actions that are Secret and below. No higher access will be granted until this council meets again to discuss your progress in a year. You will, however, be required to retain your sobriety as a condition of employment. You will submit to random checks as deemed necessary by this executive committee."

Honor nodded and nodded again. Then looked from each man to the next. "I can still work for you?"

Joseph, the man she'd never seen smile in all the times he'd been to CCS, did the absolutely unexpected. He smiled, teeth and everything. "You can, and you are."

Honor lifted her hands to her mouth. Her body went into shock. She cried, laughed, and almost fainted at the same moment. She dropped her head to her hands for a second before she popped back up again. "Oh, my God, thank you." She looked up. "Thank you. I swear I'll never give you a reason to doubt me."

Jason adjusted his tie and stood up. "I know how hard it is to maintain your sobriety, Honor. I've been where you are. It's an uphill battle, and I wish you luck. The meeting is adjourned."

The men stood and filed through a door she hadn't noticed before. Honor waited until the door shut and then let her tears fall. Her prayers had been answered. She clasped her hands together and looked up to the ceiling. "Thank you." Over-whelmed with emotion and swirling thoughts, she spun around, not knowing what to do or where to go. "Breathe," she said out loud and drew a breath. She let it out and sniffed before pulling in another, deeper breath. Letting it out, she smiled. Then she wiped her tears, spun, and headed to the big double doors she entered through, running as fast as she could. She needed to tell Sage!

20

Jewell jogged down the hall and turned left. "Right," Zane said, calling her back. She changed directions and sped down the hallway with him. "Right again." She turned, and they jogged toward the conference room where her brothers were talking to Honor. She was supposed to be in the meeting. There had been aircraft issues back home, and it took four hours to get the parts to fix whatever light or thingy was broken. The jet hauled ass to Colorado, but they were late.

"Jewell."

She stopped and swung around, almost colliding with Zane. "Sage. Did they start the meeting without me?"

"Were you supposed to be in there?" Sage asked.

"Yeah. How long has she been in there?"

"Almost ten minutes now," Smoke answered.

"Seems like forever." Sage sighed.

"It's okay. She'll be okay." Jewell knew what the verdict would be, she was told that morning right before she got on the plane, but she also knew Honor needed a friendly face at that table. Her brothers and Gabriel were not the most welcoming mugs on the planet.

The door opened behind her. Jewell twisted quickly and, when she saw who it was, rushed up to Honor and grabbed her, hugging her tightly. "The plane had mechanical problems. I was supposed to be in there for you."

Honor hugged her back. "I get to keep working for you." She started crying. "I'm so sorry for everything."

"Oh, sweetie, you've paid in spades. Everyone knows that. Don't cry anymore, or I will." Jewell started misting up. She blinked rapidly. "I wore mascara to be all professional and shit, so don't make me look like a raccoon."

"I'd like to see that," Smoke said from behind them.

Jewell groaned and muttered, "You would." She let go of Honor, who flew to Sage. Jewell smiled as they hugged. Whispered words meant only for each other couldn't be heard, and she was glad of that.

Zane wrapped an arm around her waist. "She'll be okay. I'm giving Jared credit for this one. He did the investigation and interrogation. Erik Kowalski had a lot of useful information."

"Unfortunately, all those data points need to be connected," Jewell whispered before she pulled her bottom lip in and bit it. She leaned over and spoke even quieter, watching Smoke, Sage, and Honor laugh in the hallway. "I wish Con, Brando, and Ring were fully up to speed." Guardian had recruited them, and they were halfway through the onboarding.

"A couple more months," Zane said before Smoke joined them.

"I'm going to take these two on a tour of the facility," he said.

"Secret or below only," Jewell said. She knew Honor's clearance had been stripped down to the lowest level it could be stripped and still allow her to be an asset.

"Got it. On the Candyland tour, we go." Honor waved to Jewell as Sage grabbed her hand.

Jewell leaned into her husband. "Those two are so good together."

"She needed someone to ground her." Zane kissed her hair.

"Can I interrupt?" Jared said from behind them.

Jewell turned and slugged her brother.

"Ouch, damn it, it wasn't *my* fault. I told him to wait." Jared rubbed his arm.

"Which one?" Jewell glared at her brother.

"Jason. If you hit him, I want to see it," Jared grumped.

"Where is he?" Jewell would sure as heck wallop her brother. He could have waited.

"In his office, we're doing an impromptu meeting, and they want both of you in on it."

Jewell marched through the conference room and through the door that looked like a wall. "You could have waited." She put her hands on her hips and glared at Jason.

"She was scared and nervous enough as it was. Waiting would have only made matters worse for her. Would you please sit down now and stop yelling at me?" Jason pointed to a couch in the seating area where everyone else was seated.

"Fine." Jewell knew she was right, they could have waited, but she couldn't deny Jason's argument.

She flopped onto the couch and smiled at Gabriel. "Hiya! How are you doing?"

Gabriel smiled. "I'm fine, thank you."

Jason waited for Zane and Jared to sit down before he started. "I'm concerned with the way the intelligence is developing in the Erik Kowalski interrogations."

Jared leaned forward. "The holes in the intel are so big you could shoot a basketball through each one."

"But it's worth monitoring." Joseph shifted in his chair. "Even if half of what he's alleged is true, the country will have a problem."

Everyone nodded. Jason took off his glasses. "All right. Jewell, if I didn't tell you, Con, and Brando are being expedited. Ring is the only one without the clearance we need, so you have two more assets. They'll be up and ready by Friday. Ring will have to cool his heels, and his cousins will be reminded of their NDAs."

"I'm not worried about them sharing. They're

tight-lipped and know whom they're working for. I'm pulling Ethan in on this, also." She leaned into Zane, who put his arm around her. "Honor is fast and damn good. All the honey-dos from the Dom Ops side will be routed through her. Nothing classified. A ton of work, though. We need to clear out the backlist, and that woman can fly through that just as fast as I could if I wasn't interrupted all the time with bigger issues."

"Is that a wise use of her talent?" Jacob asked.

"Well, she can't do anything for you, Joseph, or any of the higher security requests, but she can keep Dom Ops running almost singlehandedly. I'd love to get one or two others under her, so they're caught up on the regular. Those positions can be vetted quickly since they aren't top echelon clearances. The operators would be doing routine daily work for Dom Ops. Just backgrounds, searches, warrants, cameras, and such."

Jared offered, "We have room for them in the Dom Ops building in Dallas."

Gabriel interrupted, "I may have a better idea. I have an old friend who has an office building in New Orleans. I can get them offices there. That way, Honor can go in, if need be, to help set them up and clear the backlog." Gabriel shrugged. "Deacon owes me a favor or two."

"Oh, that's a lot better." Jewell clapped her hands happily. She loved that Honor would be with Sage almost all the time.

Jason put his glasses back on. "Then talk to Kannon and get him the information. He has a direct pipeline to Rio North."

"I'll do it before I leave today. Oh, I have the equipment for Honor's office purchased, and it'll ship to Sage's house as soon as you give me the go-ahead."

Jason nodded. "Do it. Zane, you're still assisting as Anubis' out-of-office point of contact, right?"

"When he needs it, yes. He's rarely unreach-able," Zane responded.

"All right, I'd like you to take over the supervi-sion of Sage Browning. He'll report to you. His independent contractors are a valuable asset, and some of them have ties to the Shadow World, so I want you to be the liaison should he need it. Joseph, you and Thanatos will be Anubis' primary backup from here on out."

"Not a problem, and it makes sense," Joseph agreed.

"Jacob, are you, Tori, and the kids settled?"

"We are. The house is beautiful. Tori has her horses, and the boys have the dirt track in the back forty. We'll be ready to go to work full-time as soon as the new operating structure is in place."

Jason nodded. "I know Talon was talking about that dirt track. Thank God you live close enough that my boys can use your death trap. It'll keep Faith from watching them on motorcycles, too."

Jacob chuckled. "We keep it safe. If anyone screws up, all privileges are revoked for three months. Everyone's privileges. So, believe me, those boys watch each other like hawks. And the security camera will catch anything they do, too."

"I hope." Jason turned to Jared. "Jared, have you and Christian made your decision?"

Jared nodded. "Christian is turning over the reins to the center. We'd like to take the residence you offered close to Jacob and you. I can drive in daily to my office in Denver. It'll take all of Guardian's presence out of DC and lower our national visibility. Guardian Security as it once was, as far as anyone can tell, is gone. We've rebranded and, with a PR campaign that I'm sending up the line, will become known as a private investigative entity that caters to a higher-class clientele."

Jason nodded and added, "Guardian Security is still federally recognized, and as of three weeks ago, we became an arm of the President of the United States. Under Executive Order, we are authorized to perform missions for the president that the other agencies with political watchdogs can't. That is classified at the highest level. The Shadows will ramp up and be utilized not only for the job they do so well but covert operations as dictated by POTUS, and as a failsafe, all missions will be approved by his closest advisers. Our overseas missions will be separated from the CIA and other intelligence agencies. We're still available to assist, but joint missions, like the mission in the Amazon that went south and our man had to salvage, won't happen again. Guardian will, for the foreseeable future, be selective of any joint missions. That still allows us cooperation and support of the other agencies and allows us to hone our skills in the direction we are heading as an organization. Welcome to the new age of Guardian Security or, as the POTUS calls us, his SPEAR."

Gabriel leaned forward. "Strategic Protection, Enforcement, and Rescue, or SPEAR, is our Guardian Security legacy, and it's in your hands.

My boys and Charlie are on board. Train them well."

"You're not retiring again, are you?" Jacob didn't laugh when he asked the question because Jewell knew that wouldn't be funny. Gabriel was their north star. Everyone needed to know he was there, guiding them.

Gabriel chuckled. "No. I'll be in your hair and fly high cover for you. But the missions and day-to-day of Guardian and SPEAR are on you. Jared, you're the CEO of Guardian Security. It has no connection that anyone is aware of to what exists here. I expect this will be one of the last times you'll see this facility. Jade and Nic, too."

"They're looking for an apartment in Denver. Neither wanted the fresh air of country living. They said they'd head to Frank's when they wanted to smell manure. But I understand and agree."

Jason leaned forward. "This is a fresh start. A new way of doing business. Going forward, things will be bumpy. We're going to iron out those items as we reach them. Legally, we're on solid ground. We're a private firm doing the bidding of the President of the United States, working with the same core values and integrity as we always have. We have checks and balances in place, so we never become part of the alphabet soup abyss strangled by red tape and political maneuvering."

"That was imperative." Gabriel nodded. "Our values have not changed. Our intent has not changed. We are Guardians to the last breath."

"Whatever it takes," Jason agreed.

"As long as it takes," Jewell and the others finished. She listened to her brothers as the meeting broke up and internalized with a clarity she rarely had during social gatherings that she'd just witnessed history in the making.

21

Sage shut the hotel door behind them and scooped up Honor, spinning her around and whooping with happiness.

She laughed and grabbed hold of him. "Stop, I'm getting dizzy!"

Sage stopped spinning, but he didn't put her down. "I'm so happy for you."

"God, I'm happy, too." She kissed him but then stopped.

He cocked his head and lowered her to the ground. "What?"

"I don't know where I'm going to live. I've never been to New Orleans, except for the drive-through when we went to your house. But, man, I was so sick then." She put her fingers to her lips and turned her head.

"Hey." Sage used his index finger to turn her attention back to him. "You'll live with me."

Honor blinked and then shook her head. "Don't you think it's too soon?"

Sage chuckled. "Name one couple you know who has been through more than the two of us in a three-month period."

Honor blinked. "Ah ... I ... I don't think I know of anyone."

"Right. We're linked together, sweetheart. My destiny and yours are welded together, and nothing will break us apart."

"Are you sure you want me to live with you? I still have a lot of issues."

Sage put his hands on her hips and started backing her up. "So do I."

"I'll have to get a car or something and find AA meetings and a sponsor." She didn't seem to realize he was backing her toward the bed.

"We'll do that the first day we're home."

"Before we left, Jewell said I could work from home for the most part after I get the New Orleans office up and running. Would that bother you?"

"Nope. If you need your own office, we'll add

on." The back of her legs hit the bed, and he tipped forward, dropping with her onto the bed.

"Mr. Browning, I sense you don't want to discuss the specifics of our living arrangements." She wrapped her arms around his neck and smiled up at him. Her beautiful blue eyes shimmered with a reflection of the exact same happiness he felt."

"Ms. Buchanan, you are a very perceptive woman." He leaned down and kissed her softly, spending time to taste and lick her lips open. He delved into her mouth, and his body sizzled with anticipation. Sage slowly undressed her. The business suit she'd worn lay in a heap somewhere besides the bed, along with his slacks and button-down. Sage ran his hands over her smooth, soft skin. Honor's curves were sexy, sensual, and his new favorite thing. He kissed down her throat, paid attention to her breasts, and started down farther.

"No, I want ..."

He lifted his head. "What do you want, babe?" Anything. He'd give her anything.

"I want to taste you." Her throat and face flushed red, either from embarrassment at the admission or excitement from their foreplay. He prayed it was the latter.

Sage laid down on the bed and shoved a pillow under his head because, holy fuck, yes, he was going to watch that happen.

Honor moved between his legs and laid down on her stomach, holding herself up on her elbows. She put her hand around his cock and stroked it. Sage groaned low in his throat. Fuck, the visual alone was going to have him spewing in seconds. Honor leaned forward and ran her tongue up the base of his cock. Hot, wet, and so soft. He shivered at the contact. Her eyes popped open, and she looked up at him. He saw the fear in her eyes. "Perfect, babe. Anything you do will be perfect. I promise."

She leaned forward again and sucked the tip of his cock into her mouth. Sage managed not to buck, but it was a close thing. Honor explored and found a rhythm between sucking him into her mouth and stroking him that punched his need up several levels. She moved between his legs, getting a bit closer before she took him farther into her mouth, his cockhead bumped the back of her throat, and she gagged a bit.

He put his hand on her cheek. "You don't have

to take in all of me." Honor hummed something while he was in her mouth, and he about died. "Shit. So close. S-so close." Sage grabbed the base of his cock and squeezed. He grabbed Honor, pulled her up his body, and lifted his legs, spreading hers. He reached down and lined himself up while taking her mouth with his. He bucked and entered her. Fuck, her heat gripped him like a glove. He rolled them and continued the kiss. He wouldn't last, but God, he'd make it up to her. He found his stride and charged up that fucking mountain. He broke the kiss, and Honor found his shoulder. She sucked hard on his skin, and the sting was blissfully intoxicating. She stopped, gasped once, and then again, and shattered under him. He dove over at nearly the same time, thrusting as he came. There wasn't enough air in the world. He dropped to his elbows, catching himself before he pancaked the woman who had changed his world. He leaned to the side and, without much effort, fell to the side, pulling her with him as he moved.

They lay together for several minutes, touching but not speaking. "Was that ... did I do okay?" she whispered.

"Okay? You drove me insane. You were

perfect." Sage pulled her into him. "We have a fresh start, babe. A new slate."

"It won't be easy. I'm still a work in progress." She ran her fingers through the light smattering of dark brown hair on his chest.

"We both are, and we'll both be learning our new places at Guardian." He ran his hand up and down her arm. Her soft skin was addictively easy to touch.

"I don't want to stay for any more hurricanes. Hard limit." She arched her back to look up at him.

"All right." He smiled. "I can live with that."

She narrowed her eyes at him. "Really?"

"Yeah, sure. We'll head up to South Dakota or visit Jewell."

"They did invite us after I get upgraded again." She shook her head. "I really thought I would be fired. I didn't tell you, but they could have pressed charges against me. I would have been guilty in the eyes of the law. I could be going to jail right now."

Sage stared down at her. "I knew."

"How?"

"Zane, I asked him at the beginning what the worst was."

"I didn't want to think about it."

"Neither did I," Sage admitted. "But we never have to think about it again."

"True. Are you sure you want to live with me? I must be exhausting." Honor pushed his hair away from his face.

"In the best possible way, babe. In the best possible way." Sage rolled over on top of her. "Care to exhaust me again?"

~

SIX MONTHS LATER:

SAGE EMPTIED HALF the bag of popcorn into the bowl, then put the diamond and sapphire engagement ring into the bowl and covered it with popcorn. He dumped his bag of popcorn into the other bowl.

Tonight was movie night. They'd started the tradition as soon as Honor had officially moved in with him. There had been bumps. Honor was a workaholic, and so was he. They learned to carve out time to be a couple and fiercely protected that time. Honor sometimes went to two meetings a day or was on her phone with her sponsor. That was a point of contention, too. That bastard Broussard had joined AA and had gotten sober. He'd apologized to Sage for all the shit he'd done to him growing up. It was part of the twelve-step process. As much as he didn't want to forgive Broussard, the man was trying. Honor saw Broussard almost every time she went to a meeting. If the guy ever said a word sidewise to the woman he loved, he'd experience a hell of a lot more than a dislocated joint.

He sat down next to her and chuckled. The temperatures in January were in the fifties, which was cold in Louisiana. Honor had acclimatized quickly because she was wearing a pair of his sweats and an old sweater of his. He loved it when she wore his clothes. They were loose and easy to peel off her.

"Here you go."

"Oh, thank you. I'm hungry, and I missed dinner again."

"I know. That's why I gave you your own bowl." She got so focused on her work that sometimes she'd forget to eat. He'd arrived home early, as was his plan, so he could pop the question during movie night. Of course, they'd made love in the shower and, for some reason, in the hallway, up against the wall. He chuckled at the hot as fuck—pun intended—thoughts that popped up.

"What are you laughing at, and what are we watching?"

"Have you ever noticed we make love in a lot of places that aren't the bedroom?"

She stopped with a couple of kernels halfway to her mouth. "Huh." She blinked. "Is that a bad thing?"

"Absolutely not. Variety is the spice of life."

"As long as there's no other feminine variety, I'm good with that. What movie are we watching."

"*Airplane*, and you're the only woman for me." He kissed her hard on the mouth and then dropped his arm over her shoulders as she leaned into him.

"I haven't watched this in eons." Honor popped more corn into her mouth.

He laughed when she did, but his attention wasn't on the movie. He heard a clink. Honor looked down at the bowl and reached in, pushing a few kernels out of the way. She reached in and picked up the ring. "What ..."

She turned to him, and he took the ring from her. "Honor Buchanan, will you marry me?"

She shook her head no. Sage's gut dropped. "N-No?" Fuck, he hadn't seen that coming.

"No, no, no ...wait ... what did you ask me?"

Defeated, he lowered the ring. "Will you m-marry me?"

Honor threw her arms around his neck, and both bowls of popcorn clattered to the floor. "Yes, God, yes!"

Sage's eyes rolled as he grabbed her and pulled her into him. "Don't ever f-fucking scare me l-like that again."

"I'm sorry. I just couldn't believe you were asking me!" She lifted away and started kissing his face in hundred different locations. He laughed and grabbed her hand. She stilled and watched as he slipped the ring onto her finger. "I don't understand how perfect my life has become." She sighed and molded into him.

Sage held her in his arms. "Our world is perfect because we exist together."

She threaded her fingers through his. He gazed at the ring he'd bought her. "Together, we're better." She sighed. "I love you."

"And I love you. But you still have to pick up the popcorn." He jumped when Honor goosed him. Their laughter rang through the house, and

Sage couldn't help but believe his mother's spirit knew he'd found the one he was destined to wait for, and she was perfect for him. The house she'd struggled to maintain and pay for was now a place of happiness and love.

EPILOGUE

Bear McGowen glanced down at his phone and smiled. Sage Browning was calling. Not texting. His new supervisor must have a job for him. "Hey, man, what's up? Am I heading out of town?"

Bear glanced out the glass walls of his office and watched as one of the newbs started to squat wrong. Casey was there in an instant, changing the stance and correcting the form. His gym had grown in reputation and popularity. He'd opened several more in neighboring cities, and he only hired the best people he could find to run the businesses.

"No, well, at least not right now." Sage's voice

came through the connection. Bear started and sat up straight. "Dude! You're not stuttering!"

"Haven't in a while. Doctors aren't as bad as they seem." Sage chuckled. "No, the reason I'm calling is ... Well, I'm getting married in December, and I want you to come."

Bear blinked and then laughed. "Count me in. Congratulations, Sage. I'm happy for you, bro."

"Thanks. I'll send the date and the hotel we're going to use. I had no idea a wedding took this much planning." The grumble in his friend's voice was amusing as hell, and he was so fucking glad he could hear it instead of the frustration that usually accompanied anything Sage tried to say. Bear had purposefully kept all conversations to text to alleviate any pain the communications would cost Sage.

"Perfect."

"You can bring a plus one. That means a date, by the way."

"Har, har, asshole." Bear rolled his eyes. "That's seven months from now. I might be able to scrounge up a woman who could tolerate me for a weekend."

"Well, if you need us to push back the date ..."

"Man, fuck you." Bear laughed and enjoyed listening to Sage's laughter in return. "Thanks for the invite. I'll block my calendar as soon as you send me the details."

"Awesome. I'll talk with you soon."

Bear disconnected and stared out at his business. He was successful, had friends throughout the community, and occasionally worked for an agency he respected beyond measure. Life was good.

His phone rang again. He glanced down at the number. He'd gotten four or five calls from the same number. No messages. Probably telemarketers. He'd finish that trend right now. He swiped the phone. "What?"

"Ah ..." A soft female voice on the other side of the line stammered. "I'm looking for Mr. McGowen."

"I don't want to buy anything." Bear snapped his response.

"I'm not selling anything. I'm calling because I think something happened to my brother."

"Who's your brother?"

"Christopher Whitehead. He said if something happened to call you." The words were rushed, and the woman sounded desperate.

Bear's body tightened; his attention fully focused on the caller at the other end of the line. He leaned forward. "You have my complete attention."

Click here for Bear's Story.

ALSO BY KRIS MICHAELS

Kings of the Guardian Series

A Backwater Blessing: A Kings of Guardian Crossover Novella

Montana Guardian: A Kings of Guardian Novella

Guardian Defenders Series

Gabriel

Maliki

John

Jeremiah

Frank

Creed

Sage

Bear

Guardian Security Shadow World

Anubis (Guardian Shadow World Book 1)

Asp (Guardian Shadow World Book 2)

Lycos (Guardian Shadow World Book 3)

Thanatos (Guardian Shadow World Book 4)

Tempest (Guardian Shadow World Book 5)

Smoke (Guardian Shadow World Book 6)

Reaper (Guardian Shadow World Book 7)

Phoenix (Guardian Shadow World Book 8)

Valkyrie (Guardian Shadow World Book 9)

Flack (Guardian Shadow World Book 10)

Ice (Guardian Shadow World Book 11)

Hollister (A Guardian Crossover Series)

Andrew (Hollister-Book 1)

Zeke (Hollister-Book 2)

Declan (Hollister- Book 3)

Hope City

Hope City - Brock

HOPE CITY - Brody- Book 3

Hope City - Ryker - Book 5

Hope City - Killian - Book 8

Hope City - Blayze - Book 10

The Long Road Home

Season One:

My Heart's Home

Season Two:

Searching for Home (A Hollister-Guardian Crossover Novel)

Season Three:

A Home for Love

STAND ALONE NOVELS

A Heart's Desire - Stand Alone

Hot SEAL, Single Malt (SEALs in Paradise)

Hot SEAL, Savannah Nights (SEALs in Paradise)

Hot SEAL, Silent Knight (SEALs in Paradise)

ABOUT THE AUTHOR

Wall Street Journal and USA Today Bestselling Author, Kris Michaels is the alter ego of a happily married wife and mother. She writes romance, usually with characters from military and law enforcement backgrounds.

Printed in Great Britain
by Amazon

23350515R00176